Jacob & Sylvia

A TALE BY TROY BLACK

Inspire Christian Books
www.InspireChristianBooks.com

TABLE OF CONTENTS

for LESLIE

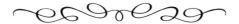

"Let no man deceive himself. If any man among you thinks that he is wise in this age, he must become foolish, so that he may become wise. For the wisdom of this world is foolishness before God. For it is written, 'He is the One who catches the wise in their craftiness.'"

1 Corinthians 3:18-19

Chapter 1: A Rainy Day

"I wouldn't say rainy days are the worst. Some people say that, but I wouldn't," said Jacob, leaning his freckled cheek against the chilly glass of his bedroom window.

It had been raining all day as if a seam had burst in the fabric of the sky and all the water had been let through. Jacob was confined to his room since his mother was out for the day, and her dog kept careful watch of the house while she was gone. Jacob had more than an overly ample aversion to the pet, and so he kept his door shut and locked when his mother was not there to keep the dog company. He just didn't like the dog jumping up into his business all the time, and he didn't think that it staying out of his room was too much to ask.

"Of course, those people probably aren't too fond of sunny days either," said Jacob. "I wish I could mix the days so that it would always be sunny in the middle of a rainy day. Then everyone would be happy or no one would. Either way, I would probably have a better chance of being allowed to play outside in the rain."

Jacob sighed and fogged up the glass all around his face. He could no longer see the backyard or the tall wooden fence that blocked his house from the rest of the neighborhood. That was fine with him. His yard was too perfect. His neighborhood was too perfect. He made sure to keep his room as messy as possible so that there would be some balance to the universe. He didn't want things getting too managed. He reasoned that if everything were too very organized, then the weathermen would always be correct. If that were true, then he would have to give up on ever having any hope that the predictions for a rainy afternoon would turn out false.

"Wait just a minute," thought Jacob. "I like the rain. What has become of me? Sitting and staring out my window has caused me to dislike something very beautiful. I should never forgive myself if I start hating rainy days, because then I would be like everyone else in the world that complain about such things. All this sitting and waiting has got to stop."

Jacob climbed down off the chair he had been kneeling on and leaned over to peer under the side of his bed. He reached as far back as he could and pulled out a big brown suitcase. Well, it wasn't that big, but it was big enough for Jacob to fit two toothbrushes, three pairs of clothes, a paper airplane, and a box of hard mints strategically inside. He stuffed these items next to one another and latched it tight. If you haven't figured it out yet, Jacob was thoroughly decided upon leaving for the afternoon. He was not just decided; he was determined.

"Let me think. Which way should I get out?" he asked himself.

You see, Jacob was an intelligent boy, and he never let circumstances (or the lack thereof) stop him from doing something he had previously determined to do. His moral clock had just about wound itself down and he was prepared to take almost any sort of punishment from his mother for leaving the house while she was away.

"It's perfect," said Jacob. "I'll go through the roof."

Though Jacob was not entirely fond of dogs (or at least the unkempt cur his mother kept), he did enjoy the company of a fish or two upon occasion. One such creature happened to be floating in a heavy glass bowl filled with water that sat on the short bookshelf along one side of his room. Now it is up to you I suppose, but if you like, you can imagine that Jacob has been unwittingly speaking to the fish this whole time.

"It won't be difficult," said Jacob, looking over his shoulder toward where his fish sat dumb and unaware of his sudden plan. "I'll simply grow my way out," he proposed.

I don't have to warn you of the silly notions young boys invent in their heads. I'm sure you are quite informed of the interminable nonsense that can ooze out of the mind of a bored child. Unaware of such a realization, Jacob was busy pouring several packets of plant fertilizer into a large cup. Once he was out of those, he ran the cup over to the fish bowl and began to tilt the bowl.

"I hope you don't mind that I need to borrow some," said Jacob as the water slowly drained over the lip. The poor fish fought to stay in the bowl and not get sucked out by the sudden current.

"That's enough," said Jacob, returning the bowl to its original position and beginning to stir the fertilizer into the water with the handle of a magnifying glass that happened to be sitting on his shelf.

He ran the cup to the center of the room and placed it in the middle of his floor.

"Any second now," Jacob told his fish, who was now downright upset about suddenly downgrading to half the size of his original living quarters.

Jacob did not seem to notice the troubled look on his fish's face. He was too busy waiting for the fertilizer to…

"Oh!" yelled Jacob. "I forgot the plant! I can't really expect something to grow out of nothing."

He hopped up onto the chair next to his window. Opening the panel just a tad, he reached out and snipped a piece of vine from the outside wall, drenching his sleeves in the process.

It was only a small strip of vine, so Jacob figured it couldn't possibly grow too very large in the small cup he had provided for it. Though, he did hope it would grow large enough for him to make his escape. He placed it carefully into the mixture of fertilizer.

"It won't be long now," he said, glancing once more over at his now severely upset pet fish.

He twiddled his fingers as he waited. Then he tapped his foot. After a few moments, he took a seat on the floor and placed his head between his hands. He slumped over and stared at the cup. Nothing happened. He sighed and lay back on the floor. Covering his face with one arm, he wondered if the fertilizer packages he had used were expired. Perhaps they were meant for flowers or elephant ears only and had no effect on plain old house-side vines. He sighed once more. Then all of a sudden he heard a popping sound. Sitting back up, Jacob leaned over the cup. Inside, he could see the liquid fizzing and mounting as the cup began to fill with foam.

"It's working," said Jacob.

Out of the foam stretched a little strand of vine, then another and another. The vines kept growing upon each other and straightening up out of the cup. They grew taller and wider until they had formed into a small bush. The roots burst out of the bottom of the cup and began to grip Jacob's carpet with their firm fingers.

"I guess that's only natural," said Jacob. "I sure hope it comes out later though."

The bush did not stop there, but it continued to expand and stretch up until it thrust its way through the roof. Bits of plaster and wood splintered down and around, almost battering the now extremely thrilled boy. Jacob leapt out of the way as a large section of his ceiling came crashing down, messily detached by the ever-thickening vine branches.

"Whoa! Mom's not going to like that," he said. "I just hope it doesn't come out of my allowance."

The trunk continued to expand even further until it

had grown so big around that it was practically taking up the whole room. Gigantic gnarled roots sprang down through the floor. The kitchen sat directly below Jacob's bedroom, and he tried not to imagine its present state. He only hoped his mother would be as understanding about this tree incident as she was every time that hideous dog tore up one of her frilly quilted cushions. At the very least, he had succeeded in creating a much friendlier habitat for do-it-yourself mushroom horticulture along his mother's kitchen counter.

"Look at the size of it!" yelled Jacob to his fish. His fish, however, did not seem to take any notice, but that was fine because Jacob never took much notice of things growing inside his fish's home either.

Now if you see yourself as an intelligent being, you might be thinking to yourself, "Plants don't grow through roofs of children's bedrooms, especially not as quickly as all that." If this is the case, then I would agree that you have some merit to your feelings, however, I would not agree that you are so very intelligent considering what you have just read about a plant doing the very thing you disagree with. So now that we have straightened that out, I will continue with the story.

Jacob picked up his suitcase, saluted his American-flag-patterned bed sheets, and began to climb the side of the large trunk. Though mostly unfamiliar with the ways of large-scale greenery and perennial plant life, Jacob thought the bark of the tree reminded him of something in particular. Supposing he had considered the question in mind for longer than a moment, he would have recognized the similarities between it and an ordinary tree from the genus Quercus. Though I say "ordinary," I do not mean to belittle the giant tree. For this Giant happened to be a monstrous cousin to the oak, stretching more than fifteen miles high.

It was hard to climb at first, but as he made it to the third branch Jacob found that there were branches growing out of it in every which way, which allowed him to mount the tree at a very quick pace. Poking his head through the top of his house, he surveyed the neighborhood. In all the excitement, he had forgotten to check if the rain had stopped, but he now realized that it certainly had. The sun was out, and a winding rainbow now drifted from one side of the sky to the other. Between the colors ordinarily expected from an after shower rainbow, it almost seemed as if a magnificent golden arc shone through, radiating in little beams of light across the stratosphere.

"I wonder if I could reach it," Jacob thought, grabbing hold of the next branch.

As he kept climbing, he realized that the tree had grown several times larger than he had originally estimated. In fact, he could hardly even see the top considering how it grew all the way up into a large cloud. He kept moving upward, though he began to feel a little dizzy and very lonely so high above the landscape. His neighborhood was soon nothing but a checkered pattern of brown and green squares with little black lines leading through them, and no one could have spotted him from that far down even if they had wanted to. Occasionally a bird would float on by and Jacob would politely address it and ask if the weather was always this lovely at such a high altitude, but strangely enough, he had quite a difficult time trying to acquire a response. At one point, he nearly lost his footing and would have fallen to his death if he had not quickly grasped a large tuft of ruffled fungi emerging out of the side of the tree.

"That was a close one," said Jacob. Then he realized that his fish was no longer within hearing range, and he felt rather ashamed for speaking out loud with no one around. "I shall be more careful about where I place my feet," he thought.

Arriving finally in a vast cloudbank, Jacob stopped to rest. If he had not just climbed several miles, he could have believed that he was only about twenty feet off the ground on a rather foggy afternoon. He set up his suitcase on the branch next to him and quickly opened it. The effort that climbing such an extreme height demanded was more than such a boy was ordinarily used to exerting, and he had grown frightfully hungry.

"Oh how I wish I had packed something to eat," he thought.

Scrounging through the pockets inside the case, he found a small packet of peanuts from the last time he had taken a flight with his mom to see his grandparents. He quickly ate most of the packet before remembering how his mother had told him that he needed to eat slower, and so then he ate the last three halves in as deliberately slow of a manner as he could possibly manage. He also hoped they would be more filling that way.

After that, he tried to take a short nap. Soon however, he felt hungry again. He was startled awake by a sound, which reminded him of the tractor races he used to watch while at his grandparents old house. Then he realized that it wasn't so much like a tractor but more like a plane. The fog had lifted somewhat and Jacob could see a few long figures approaching in the distance, their engines roaring louder and louder as they neared. The first one passed by, and Jacob realized that it wasn't one of the large passenger planes that he had ridden in before. These were smaller, two-man aircraft. Jacob was so focused on the plane that had just flown by, that he failed to notice how incredibly close the path of the second plane was to the tree. As it passed by, its wing clipped one of the branches next to the one Jacob was on, and it rebounded back toward him. Smacking him firmly in the middle of his diaphragm, the branch sent Jacob flying through the misty air. Now, I use the term 'flying' to mean something completely different from the flying the planes were doing, for the flying that Jacob was taking part in was much more like falling. This would have frightened him immensely if he had been given the chance to ponder the event, but he was soon caught on the wing of the third plane and lifted hastily away from the tree.

"I shall miss that suitcase dreadfully," thought Jacob. "I can't imagine finding another toothbrush with such panache way up here." Jacob thought the word 'panache' quite loosely, and some would even say incorrectly, for he really did not refer to a tuft of feathers or a display of self-confidence.

He had simply overheard his mother using the word in a similar situation and decided that it was time he developed some sense of sophistication and knowledge of vocabulary. However, if asked, he would have admitted that he could have picked a better time.

"What on earth?" said a voice from the cockpit.

Jacob looked over to find a man curiously peaking up at him from under the wing of the plane.

"Grab my hand!" the man shouted over the engine's roar.

Jacob did as he was told and scooted over until the man was able to pull him down into the plane.

"How on earth did you get on top of our plane?" asked the man, sitting back down in the passenger's seat at the small cockpit. There were two men. One was flying the plane, and the other one (who had just rescued Jacob), seemed to be doing nothing.

"I fell out of a tree," said Jacob, taking a seat on a coarse, wooden box behind them.

"You fell out of a tree?" asked the pilot, as if he had heard wrong. "I never would have imagined we were flying at a height where it would be possible to catch children falling out of trees. What altitude are we at now?"

"It says we're just at sea level right now," answered the co-pilot.

"Sea level?" asked Jacob. "Doesn't that mean we should be hitting the ground any time now?"

"No, that's ground level," said the pilot. "I can still see so we are definitely at see level right now."

"He didn't say see level, he said *sea* level," said Jacob.

"Yes, that's nice," the man replied, obviously uninterested in the opinion of a small child, even a child as intelligent in appearance as Jacob. "All I know is that I'm never flying at this height again if we're likely to run into falling children. My mother said that no matter what I did with my life, if I listened to her, I would always keep my feet on solid ground. That's why I like flying at ground level and not an inch higher."

"But that's ridiculous," said Jacob. "You aren't really flying if you're still on the ground."

"What do you know about flying?" the pilot asked, rhetorically. "What's your name, kid?"

Both men seemed sort of odd to Jacob. He was scared to give away his real name because there was no telling what sort of fellows he had climbed aboard a plan with, so he searched around and found the word 'Darnish' printed in bold letters on several large crates behind him.

"My name is Darnish," he replied, only afterward realizing the dull nature of his choice of fabrication.

"Darnish? Well fancy that," said the co-pilot. We happen to be delivering a whole plane full of darnishes at this very moment."

"That sure is strange," added the pilot. "And where are you from, Darnish?"

Jacob looked around again to try and cover up his identity once more. Printed under the word 'Darnish' on the boxes was an address that included the word 'Rumshire,' so he made use of that word as well, this time feeling quite certain that the two pilots would not catch on.

"I'm from Rumshire," he said.

"Rumshire? Really?" asked the co-pilot. "What are the odds of that? These darnishes were made in Rumshire and we just left from there not two days ago."

"Well, that is quite a strange coincidence," said the pilot. "I just have one more question for you," he said, turning to peer inquisitively at Jacob. "What is your favorite word in the whole universe?" He raised one eyebrow, intently expressing a growing feeling that eluded Jacob's train of thought.

Jacob was stumped. He had no idea what his favorite word might be, because he had never thought of it before. He thought it might be safe to say any word that came to mind, but then he remembered what he had heard about the subconscious's ability for being cruel at the most inopportune times. He felt that instead of risking his identity in the slightest, he would once again search around for something that he could pass of as his favorite word in the universe. On the side of the plane wall, printed in rather grossly huge letters, was the word 'Francesco.'

"Well, I think I would have to say, Francesco," answered Jacob.

This really tipped the cake. The co-pilot began raving about something frightfully horrid and the pilot dove into a riled rant over something similar in subject matter.

"What's the matter?" cried Jacob, baffled by their sudden strange and frightful behavior.

"Do you realize what you just said?" asked the co-pilot, in a state of shock.

"I just told you my favorite word in the universe," said Jacob, attempting to speak some relief into the clamor. "I can't see the harm in that."

"Well, that would have been fine and all, except for one thing," said the co-pilot. "That word just happens to be the name of the plane we're flying in at this very moment."

"So what?"

"Don't you see?" asked the pilot. "Everything you just said was so entirely coincidental that it wasn't."

"I don't follow," said Jacob.

"The name, the city, and your favorite word in the universe all had something to do with what we are doing at this very moment. I don't like to be superstitious, but anyone could see that you've put us in a tight spot."

"I hate to say it, but he's right," said the pilot. "There isn't any getting around it. We have to throw you out."

"Throw me out?" asked Jacob, his eyes widening with incredulity. "How on earth did you come to that conclusion?"

"Well, if you aren't around to remind us of these strange coincidences, then its more or less likely that they didn't happen at all," explained the co-pilot patiently, with a tone in his voice that made Jacob feel as if he should have already known this. "I am sorry that it has to come to this."

"So am I," gulped Jacob as the co-pilot pushed him up next to the open door.

"Happy landings," said the pilot. "We hope to forget about you soon, kid."

"Same here," said Jacob.

"Oh yes, you might need this," said the co-pilot, handing Jacob a backpack parachute.

Jacob felt a calming wave of relief rush through his pounding heart as he tightened the harness and prepared to jump.

"Hopefully this will teach you not to be so coincidental. It's just plain scary," said the co-pilot as he pushed Jacob out of the plane.

Jacob fell quickly. He didn't feel like he was flying this time. As he glanced around the landscape below, he realized that they had come into a mountainous terrain. Peaks were sticking up toward him here and there. He would have to be extra careful in his landing. He looked back up toward the plane just in time to see it smash suddenly into the side of a massive mountaintop that had sat in their path. A blisteringly brilliant explosion burst from the side of the rock as the plane went up in flames so fast that it nearly disappeared. However, something odd seemed to happen in the split second that the plane exploded. Jacob almost thought that he could see a dark whiff of cloud whipping through the wreckage.

Jacob went stiff with shock. His senses came back in a rush. He inhaled sharply, realizing he was still hundreds of feet above the ground and free-falling towards it.
"I didn't like those two much anyway," he thought, trying to make himself feel a little better. "Hopefully I'll find better company after I land."

Now, at the moment you might be thinking, "Why did the pilots have to die? And why so suddenly at that?" To answer your question, I should first inform you that the two pilots were illegally delivering contraband materials that would lead young children astray, eventually causing them to lead upsettingly horrid lives of malice and mischief.

This should not really make a difference about your feelings concerning their death but I am confident enough in the hypercritical state of the mind to make the guess that it nonetheless does. Also, the characters were shallow at best, and so they really had little development left to explore. This being the case, the only viable option was to kill them off suddenly without remorse. There were other options available, but I doubt you would care enough about them by now for it to make any difference. With that being said, if you do happen to come across other such characters with little prospect for expansion, you can probably expect them to face a similarly cruel and thoughtless fate.

I do not want to make it seem as if Jacob experienced no remorse, for the truth about the matter is that he did, and though he felt awful about the sudden loss of the two pilots, Jacob knew that he had to act quickly if he himself were to survive. He pulled the string on the side of the strap-on parachute pack, and out from it flew an anvil on the end of a rope. It fell so forcefully, that Jacob somehow began falling at an even quicker rate than before.

"Well, that is no good at all," said Jacob. "It also doesn't make much sense that my chute is heavier now than it previously was."

He looked down at the strap of the parachute pack, and he found a curious label printed next to a knob in the fabric. It read 'Anti-Parachute Pack.'

"That explains it," he remarked to himself.

He switched the knob so that it would reverse, and the anvil quickly detached and fell away. Out from the pack formed an enormous multicolored chute that caught Jacob up in a swirl of movement. He felt suddenly stopped in the air, and he began to slowly drift upon the evening breeze into a frozen gust.

"I-i-i-i-i-t-s g-e-e-e-e-e-t-i-i-i-i-i-i-n-g r-a-a-a-a-t-h-e-r c-o-o-o-l-d o-u-t h-e-e-e-r-e," chattered Jacob, beginning to shiver.

As he lowered closer and closer to the ground, his

parachute carried him over a few shorter mountains and into a valley between several rocky ridges. He could see a scattered display of lights reflecting off of several metallic surfaces in the side of the mountain, though it was difficult to make out what it was he was actually witnessing due to the dense fog that blanketed the landscape. Suddenly, his strap caught above him on a hanging metal grate. He hung there awkwardly until he noticed a platform not very far to his left. Swinging back and forth by the ropes of the chute, he was able to grab the raised edge of the platform, pulling himself to safety. It was now too dark to figure out where he was, so he pulled on the chute until it came loose and then wrapped himself in it for warmth. Soon he was fast asleep.

Chapter 2: A Rocket Ship

The morning came quicker than expected due to an alarming sound, which startled Jacob senseless. Rubbing his eyes, he peered around. The whole valley was filled with machinery and buildings covered in pipes and platforms. He assumed he was at the very top of the tallest building because he could see everything else from where he sat.

"What an oddly shaped structure," thought Jacob. "There doesn't seem to be a way inside (or down for that matter)."

As he stood up, his parachute started to blow away in the wind. Fortunately, it was still attached to his back and it couldn't get far. Then the crazy alarm rang once more.

"What on earth could it mean?" he asked himself.

Just then, an electronic sounding voice began counting down through a series of large speakers in the side of the mountain.

It announced, "Liftoff in: TEN, NINE, EIGHT, SEVEN, SIX…"

Jacob didn't want to think about what was coming next. All he knew was that it couldn't be good. Examining the building on which he sat once more, he realized that he had slept at the top of an enormous rocket launch pad. The countdown finished and liftoff began. Jacob watched as the curved wall next to him began traveling upward in the air. In sudden desperation, he latched his arms as firmly as he could around a metal bar on the grating. Unfortunately, the top of his parachute snagged a latch on the side of the rocket and it dragged him up into the air after it. Jacob screamed as the platform grew smaller and smaller below him. It would have been his end had he not been able to swing around and grab a dislodged panel on the rocket surface, to which he intensively held on for dear life.

"This is not good at all," he thought, as he imagined his brains getting beaten to pudding inside his head. He felt like he was going to be sick. Every once in a while he would look down and be able to see less and less of the mountainous terrain. Oddly enough, it reminded him of the move that he and his mother had made two summers before. In a way, it was like he was once more being driven down the stretch of dirt road for the last time, watching the white picket fence grow smaller and smaller. Soon, the whole landmass below him appeared less like the ground and more like a rather large orb smothered in green and blue plaster, and the clouds formed into what looked to be foaming tides, frozen in a moment of time.

"Well, I've never been to outer space," he thought. "This should be quite the experience. I hope my mom understands, though. Sometimes she isn't too keen on me going places I haven't already been. Of course, if I always followed that rule, then I would never be anywhere new, and that might get old rather quickly."

As he looked up, he could see that they were making a sudden approach toward a wall of light. To Jacob's surprise, a hatch burst ajar not feet from where he clung tightly, and a man reached down and pulled Jacob inside.

"Another fortunate save," said Jacob breathlessly. "I was beginning to worry."

"What's that?" asked the man, who wore an orange jumpsuit and had a thick similar-colored headband squeezed round his brow.

"Oh, nothing," said Jacob.

"What on earth were you doing out there?" asked the man.

"Well I didn't *mean* to be there, if that's what you think," Jacob replied. "I just got a little caught up in the moment. The whole thing was completely unforeseen if you can believe it."

"Well, no harm done, I suppose," said the man. "I guess you should know my name then. I'm Hanson."

"It's a pleasure to meet you, Hanson," said Jacob. He was still worried about giving his identity away to a stranger so he used the same fake name as before, forgoing the thought that such a deception had previously proved hazardous. "I'm Darnish," he said.

"Nice to meet you, Darnish," said Hanson. "Listen, I've got to check a few things back here, but if you want to head up to the front I'm sure Chandler and Susan can find somewhere for you to sit. They might even be able to get some food going."

This sounded great to Jacob, who had not eaten anything since the package of peanuts the day before. As soon as Hanson was gone, Jacob tried walking to the next room, but he instead found himself once again at odds with the unordinary and out-of-place. He, at first, thought that he had tripped, but then he fell upward instead of down. Jacob felt his cheeks flush with embarrassment. He could not believe that he had forgotten that you can float around in a space ship, but then again, he had not had time to really think much about it. He bounced from wall to wall, shoving himself as hard and far as he could. The rooms were small and oddly shaped, and the walls were covered in white metal panels and wires and small beams. Jacob made sure not to ram anything that looked important. He was moving along, exhilarated and undisturbed, until something strange caught his eye. What appeared to be a black figure rushed by the entrance to the room on his right.

"Hanson?" asked Jacob. "Is that you?"

Now I will answer Jacob's question before the story continues because it does in fact involve a bit more explanation than you may have assumed. What Jacob had seen, though briefly so, was not Hanson at all. You might be thinking, "Well I had already guessed as much on my own." I will warn you that thoughts like this can get you into trouble while reading such a story, because at any moment I have the ability to say anything about you that I want and you will never have the proper chance to retort. This being said, it would be best if you keep your assumptions to yourself and just read on.

Before I continue though, I would like to warn you about what it was that Jacob had actually glimpsed out of the corner of his eye. If you are altogether familiar with the term "antagonist," then you should understand at once. If not, then I will explain. What Jacob had noticed happens to be the Villain to this tale. Now you might think, "Well it's about time that a villain appears," but I will warn you once more. Don't assume anything about this villain that you would about ordinary villains. I will be as clear as possible. At the end of this story, the villain wins. He ends up getting the best of Jacob. Now, this might be rather early in the story to be revealing to you the ending but that just goes to show that I trust you with this important information and I expect you to keep it secret. You must understand, if Jacob knew what was going to happen, he may have thought twice about embarking on such an adventure at all.

There came no reply so Jacob continued on. Pulling himself up through a narrow chute, he arrived at what looked to be a fancy sort of control room. A man and woman (also dressed in orange jumpsuits) were startled by his entrance. Nevertheless they found him a seat behind them on a not-sosnug little chair that popped out of the floor at the command of a few buttons, and they even offered him something to eat. Jacob felt the need to explain to the two strangers how he became a stowaway to their expedition.

"So what are you all exploring?" asked Jacob excitedly after explaining.

"What do you mean?" asked the man named Chandler.

"You have to have a mission of some kind," Jacob expounded. "They don't send people to space for no reason at all."

"Well, that's sort of a touchy subject," said Chandler, averting his eyes to the control panel in front of him.

"Come on Chan, he's just a kid. It doesn't really matter," said Susan.

"Yeah I guess not," said Chandler. "Well kid, we are on a mission to rescue a lost ship named Conquistador Seven that crash-landed somewhere on the back side of the moon. Two brave astronauts were caught by surprise when a meteor shower came out of nowhere and hit their ship. There has been no communication since the accident, but we haven't given up hope."

"That is an honorable mission," said Jacob, with a smile. "I am glad to be a part of it. If there's anything you want me to do to help just let me know."

"Will do, kid," said Chandler good-naturedly.

Jacob was just about to bite into a strange looking piece of what he assumed was dried meat, when Hanson's voice echoed from the halls behind.

"Hey Chandler! Can you and Susan come help me for a moment? I think there's something wrong with this oxo-conversion valve!"

"On our way!" answered Chandler.

"But if we go help him, then who is going to fly the ship?" asked Susan. "The sensors say that we'll be reaching the moon in less than a few minutes, and the beginning signs of a meteor shower are appearing on radar at this very moment."

She finished her statement with a touch of worry in her voice.

"Well, Darnish can fly it," said Chandler brightly. "He offered to help if we needed him. You can fly the ship, right Darnish?"

"I've never done anything like that before," answered Jacob. "But I'm rearing to give it a try if you'll let me." Jacob felt a little uneasy but flattered at having received such an offer. The strange thought that what he was about to do was a very bad idea and that these adults were not so intelligent as they seemed passed briefly through his mind, and then he took one look at the master control panel covered in flashy lights and levers and forgot all about his consternation.

"Yeah, it is easy," said Chandler. "Just steer with this lever thingy and push these little buttons here when… necessary. They *should* all be labeled correctly."

"Okay!" said Jacob, jumping up out of his chair and taking a hold of what resembled a joystick, only much larger.

"Just don't run into anything," Chandler laughed merrily as he and Susan left the control room.

They were in deep space now, and there really wasn't much around that Jacob could possibly crash into except for a large round rock-like planet directly in front of him. Jacob figured that it must have been the moon, even though it didn't look much like it from where he was sitting.

"Let's see," Jacob thought, giving the side of his noggin a good scratch. "They said the other ship crashed on the far side of the moon, so I guess I'll just head in that direction."

He pulled the lever to one side and the ship began to move slowly around the moon. After only a few minutes, he could see the meteor shower that had been predicted by the ship's sensors.

"That looks pretty intense," thought Jacob, as a few beads of sweat begin to form on his brow.

He figured it wouldn't be too hard to wiggle his way through the shower though, so he steered into it at full speed, assuming that the crew would be returning at any moment to take over. It was easy at first. There weren't many rocks passing by, so he was able to dodge most of them. Sometimes, the smaller ones impacted the side of the rocket, but he guessed that it wouldn't harm the ship too much. The panels had appeared fairly sturdy when he had been dangling outside. Just when he thought he was through, as seems to be the universal pattern in such cases, a rather large meteor happened to appear out of nowhere and crash into the side of the ship. Jacob was shaken from his seat. The dials on the dashboard were violently flittering one direction and the other. Overhead lights flashed on and off and alarms buzzed. Then a computer-like voice could be heard.

It stated, too calmly for the emergency at hand, "Airlock disabled. Abandon ship. Airlock disabled. Abandon ship."

Suddenly, a corner of the control room was ripped open like a pressured seam and space began to suck everything out of the room. Jacob reached down and wrapped his fingers through the grate on the floor, but his strength soon gave out. Perhaps if he had had the chance to eat something more he would have been able to hang on a few moments longer, but it was no use. He rolled out into space along with the rest of the parts of the ship. Jacob was scared. He felt abandoned in a cavernous and desolately bare part of the universe. Huge twisted pieces of metal from the now destroyed rocket floated by. Jacob worried that he would be stuck there forever, but then he realized that he couldn't breathe and that he would probably die of suffocation at any second.

"Well, I've got to have an idea of some kind…" he thought.

Looking down, he realized that he was wearing his pump-up air basketball shoes.

"Perfect," he thought.

He reached into his pocket and pulled out a small pocketknife. With one small puncture in each shoe, he was off. He pointed his toes and began to fly toward the moon.

Unfortunately Jacob wasn't the best at holding his breath and with each moment he felt weaker and weaker, his perception becoming continually fuzzier.

Now, you must understand that Jacob was in no position to be thinking clearly, so it never occurred to him that he would have had no better chance of survival even if he had reached the moon. Of course, if he had realized this and given up, then he would have died then and there in the lonely dark of outer space.

"Just a little further," he thought, as he floated along.

Jacob awoke to a blurry, bearded face hanging over him. He sat up and asked where it was that he happened to be.

"You're on the Conquistador Seven," came the reply. "You're lucky that we saw you. You didn't look to be in very good shape. I guess someone out there's watching over you, my lad." As his vision cleared, Jacob perceived that his savior was a very scraggly and dirty individual indeed.

"I guess so," said Jacob. "You said this is the Conquistador Seven? I thought that ship wrecked on the backside of the moon."

"It did, and now here we are two years later. The Conquistador was designed to be a moon base, and my wife and I were able to set up most of the working functions of the ship after it crashed. Unfortunately all of our communication was corrupted upon impact. So now we are just sitting and waiting for rescue here on the backside of the moon."

"I see," said Jacob. "Well, I don't mean to intrude, and I don't feel too shook up now that I've had a chance to rest, so I guess it's about time I get going. Just how do you get out of this place anyway?"

Jacob took a better look at the room in which he sat.

He didn't see much point in sticking around. The place looked completely dilapidated, showing no inclination of homey furnishings or common pleasantries. He was sitting on a broken cargo bed in a small compartment room that only had a single rusty lamp hanging above for light. The hall leading out of the room was just about pitch black, and cables and panels hung down from the ceiling. The man with the beard laughed.

"Oh there isn't any way out," he said. "It looks like you'll be stuck here as long as we are, kid."

Jacob did not like the sound of that. You see, he was rather fond of new places, but even the most adventurous locations grew boring to him after a while. He thought about being stuck with the bearded man and his wife for the rest of his life in a small dark space station. Then he envisioned himself with a beard. Something about the thought gave him the chills. Now, I understand that chills can be a very good experience in some circumstances, but I guarantee that this was not such a case.

"Levi, don't go getting him down like that," came a voice from the hall.

A middle-aged woman with rose-colored hair and kind eyes emerged from the darkness. Her skin was also smeared with dirt and grease.

"There is a way," she continued steadily, "But it's risky."

"Darla, you wouldn't make him go through that," said Levi.

"I didn't say we would make him. But if he wants out, then we should give him the option. Who knows what could happen?"

"Well, I guess it can't hurt to show him," responded Levi, and they exchanged a hopeful look that Jacob did not understand.

"Hang on," interrupted Darla. "Let me find him something to eat first. He looks starved."

Jacob followed Darla down the dark hall and into a room resembling a walk-in closet where she pulled a large tray out of the wall. Jacob noticed that the grated floor had turned to squishy mush beneath his feet. He didn't know what it was he was standing in but he knew he didn't like it. Darla tore off a section of a strange substance in the tray and handed it to Jacob. He unwrapped it to find a chalky, white mixture that tasted like cereal but melted like candy in his mouth.

"It's oatmeal," said Darla as she led him into the next room.

Jacob was normally fond of oatmeal, and this strange approximation of it was no exception.

"So you're looking for a way out?" asked Levi, looking up from a keyboard that he had been punching numbers into.

The room was shaped like a large donut, with a cylindrical machine in the center. There were four hallways leading out in different directions, and they were all just as pitch black as the rest of the ship. A bright light illuminated the room from the floor of the machine in the middle. The walls of the machine were somewhat transparent, and several mechanical boxes and wires were situated around them.

"What is this?" Jacob asked, feeling an ounce more uncertain than before.

"Well, believe it or not," began Levi. "It's a teleportation device."

"You mean like a teleporter?" asked Jacob, and he then quickly stated with certainty, "I'm pretty certain those haven't been invented yet."

"Of course they haven't," said Levi. "That's why I had to invent this one myself. When me and my wife realized that there was no way to return home, and that it wasn't very likely that our "friends" from the station would be rescuing us, I decided to take matters into my own hands."

"But they did come to rescue you," replied Jacob. "That's how I got here. I rode with them in their rocket."

"Yes, and now they're all dead, God rest their souls," said Levi. "And we will be soon if we can't get this thing working."

"How come?" Jacob asked, defiantly.

"Oh just be quiet," said Darla. "Don't go telling the poor kid ghost stories and scaring him for no reason."

"No, I want to know. What are you afraid of?" Jacob asked, his voice trailing off as he looked uneasily at their terrified appearance.

"Levi comes up with all sorts of crazy ideas. That's what happens when you're cramped up in such a small spot for so long. You start believing anything your imagination tries to throw at you."

"It wasn't my imagination," said Levi. "*I know what I saw.*"

"What was it?" asked Jacob, now feeling compelled to find out what it was that made them seem so troubled.

Darla rolled her eyes and sat down to work on her cross-stitch.

"Well," whispered Levi, "I was working in the engine room one day when the lights went out. There was a malfunction of some sort, but I didn't really think much of it. Anyway, as I was trying to reroute the power, I heard something in the dark behind me. When I turned around, I caught sight of a black…something in the darkness. It was almost like a shadow covered in black robes. I was so frightened that I couldn't bring myself to move no matter how hard I tried. Fortunately for me, the lights came back on and the creature retreated into the darkness as quickly as it had come."

"So you think there's something like that in the space station somewhere?" asked Jacob.

"Not only is it here, but I think its just waiting for us to run out of power so that it can slink back out of the darkness and kill us."

"Fiddlesticks," said Darla. "There's no such thing. You were only imagining it. I'm telling you. Levi, sometimes you go too far. Scaring a kid like this is just not right."

"I wasn't scaring him, I was warning him," Levi insisted. "Don't listen to her. She just doesn't want to believe it. At first, I didn't want to either, and I would not have – except that I've caught sight of it on several occasions."

"So why are you still here then?" asked Jacob. "Why can't you use the teleportation device to just go home? Doesn't it work?"

"No, it works…I think," said Levi. "The problem is that I haven't had the time to test it yet."

"Tell him the truth," said Darla, looking over at Jacob with a slightly embarrassed look on her face. "The truth is, neither of us are willing to use it."

"Okay, okay," admitted Levi, shaking his shoulders and smiling awkwardly. "I was sort of hoping, that if you really wanted a chance at getting home, that you would be willing to give it a try. I wouldn't force you to do it if you didn't want to. We just haven't had the guts to try it."

"Yeah, of course I'll try it!" shouted Jacob, jumping at the opportunity to teleport. "How come ya'll are scared of trying it out?"

"Well, we don't know where it would go exactly, and I'm not sure if the test subject would actually…well, survive."

Questions surrounding life and death hung but a moment on the forefront of Jacob's mind. I really do not know for sure what it was that allowed Jacob to once more risk his life so easily. Perhaps it was his young age or perhaps his inexperience with loss. The difficulty with understanding Jacob and his motives is that he had lost more than he could remember. Something that Jacob may learn by the end of this tale is that loss is not always measured accurately without a proper understanding of what one has gained, and that just because something is gone does not necessarily mean that it is lost. Of course it is not up to me to say what Jacob will learn.

"Heck, I'll take that risk," Jacob remarked with a glance around his dank and dusty surroundings, "It's better than being cooped up in here for the rest of my life."

Levi was pleasantly surprised that Jacob was so willing to test out his machine. He eagerly powered it up and set the parameters so that Jacob would hopefully end up somewhere on earth. The machine took a few minutes to configure, so

Darla packed Jacob some strips of astronaut food for his journey. Levi handed Jacob a small flashing device. When all was ready, Jacob stepped through the large glass door and stood excitedly above the blue light panel on the floor. He was enclosed in a sort of capsule in the middle of the room, able to see out in every direction.

Levi had to yell through the glass so that Jacob could hear him. "Now, when you arrive, there will be only a few seconds to press the button on that device! It will send a short signal back through the portal hole allowing us to see the location of your arrival!"

"Got it!" yelled Jacob, examining the strange device. It was a spherical-shaped glowing gadget covered with little hexagons, and on top was a single button.

The machine grew very hot and several other lights turned on, causing Jacob to have a difficult time seeing out of the glass.

"It's working!" shouted Levi excitedly from outside. "Just a few seconds longer!"

What Levi had failed to realize though, was that the power the machine drew to itself caused a shortage to the rest of the station. A sudden power drop threw out the lights around the entire ship. The only lights left shining were the bright rings of light coming from the machine in the center of the room. The room went silent, and then the machine began rumbling with a surging roar. Oddly however, the air around Jacob began to feel colder.

"Levi?" yelled Jacob, suddenly afraid, "Is this supposed to happen?"

Jacob neared the glass and attempted to shield his eyes from the glare. Levi and Darla were nowhere to be seen. Jacob peered down the hall that stretched away from that side of the room. He figured it was just his imagination, but it almost seemed like the darkness was slowly growing out of the hall and expanding into the room. He ran to the other side of the machine and peered out. Levi and Darla were not there either. Where could they have gone? Then, without warning, a sight that seemed to resemble a face appeared on the other side of the glass. Jacob leapt back and fell down onto the blue light issuing out of the floor. He looked up to discover a black mist hovering all around the machine. It flowed around the glass, almost as if the light of the machine kept it out. Then everything went white.

Chapter 3: A Beautiful Princess

Jacob opened his eyes but could not see anything. He rubbed them several times and slowly his vision returned. He felt the ground beneath him. It was soft and wet. It was difficult to make out the shapes around him. They were tall and brown, and there were large green spots all around. Nothing would come into focus, no matter how hard he tried to adjust his eyes. Then he remembered. He needed to hit the button.

"Where is it?" he asked himself, fumbling around.

He felt something hard and round. Picking it up, he pushed what felt like a button several times just to make sure it worked. A few hundred thousand miles away, a message was received by nothing but a lonely space station, empty and dark. Jacob was sure that his mission was done, so he discarded the small contraption and began wandering around even before his eyesight restored to full functionality. As soon as he was able to see clearly, he realized he was in the middle of a large forest filled with the oddest sorts of trees and shrubs. The grass grew as tall as he was, and everything else looked bigger than average as well. The trees curved over as if someone very heavy had gone around climbing each of them in pursuit of dates or coconuts or something else that often grows at the tops of trees. Except for the fact that he was in the middle of a forest, and that the trees leaned this way and that, the style of plant life would have ordinarily caused him to assume that he was in close proximity to a beach.

"Which way now?" he thought, taking a long look around and seeing nothing but forest in every direction.

"Hello!" he yelled, hoping that someone would hear him and reply.

After a few seconds, a rustling began in the grass in front of him. Out from behind a layer of tall brush flittered a pale yellow butterfly that seemingly cast powder as it flew. The strange thing about it was that it also seemed to change in size. At first he thought it was getting smaller, but then he realized that such a thought was a fairly ridiculous notion. Making up his mind, Jacob followed it for a handful of minutes until he came to the edge of a cliff. Several hundred feet below, a river raged at the bottom of a thin gorge. The walls on either side dripped with the same shrubbery and vines that filled the whole forest.

"Hercules!" shouted Jacob into the gorge.

'Hercules' echoed back several times over until it faded away.

"That was sick!" exclaimed Jacob. "I wish we had one of these in our back yard."

You may be questioning Jacob's use of the word 'sick,' so I should inform you that in this instance he meant it to describe a feeling of immersive excitement. You could almost use it as a synonym for the word 'awesome.'

You may also be wondering why Jacob shouted the word 'Hercules,' and not the words 'echo' or 'district attorney' or simply 'hey.' I regret to say that I have no satisfactory answer for you. I can only guess that no one really understands what goes through the mind of a young boy

Jacob's age. Oh, that's right. I have not previously mentioned his age, so you could really be sort of confused at the moment. Well, let's just say that he is at the age where a young boy begins to like girls but he doesn't yet admit it to himself. This may be important to the rest of the story, so don't forget it.

Anyhow, Jacob followed the princess until she led him to a rather large city. Goodness, now I've somehow skipped ahead of myself. This is what happens when I have to stop to explain things to you. From now on, I'm just going to assume that you know what the heck is going on. And if you don't, you really aren't very imaginative are you? But in order to be civil I will back up to where we were.

Jacob continued to stare down the gorge until his eyes could stare no longer. This was fine with him because his attentions were suddenly drawn elsewhere by a girlish giggling from the bushes behind him. He spun around to just catch sight of a small human figure dashing off into the forest. He obeyed his first instinct, which was to run after the figure. It was hard going at first and he soon realized that whomever it was that he was pursuing was faster than him. Eventually he stopped to catch his breath.

"What are you doing?" came a voice from out of the brush.

"Breathing," answered Jacob. "You just about wore me out."

"How come?" asked the voice. "I wasn't really running very fast at all. I think you just don't run enough."

"Well that might be the case," said Jacob. "Either way, I don't think you should be too hard on me. I'm a middle class, suburban-dwelling, video-game-enthusiast. I don't think you should expect someone like me to be quite so quick as someone like you."

"What do you mean someone like me?" asked the voice.

"Well, you obviously live out here in the middle of nowhere. You're used to the exercise. I bet you have to fend for yourself, catch wild animals, and run from danger. I mean, you ran from me well enough."

"Well, you didn't look very dangerous," said the voice. "I only wanted to have a little fun."

A young girl who appeared to be about Jacob's age stepped out from behind a leaf her own size. Her head tilted down a bit, but Jacob could still see the kindness in her gaze. The line of her face was solid yet beautiful and her golden brown hair complimented her wide brown eyes. She had a slender body adorned by a ruffled purple dress fit for a princess.

"How on earth were you running so fast in high heels?" asked Jacob in astonishment.

"Practice," she answered. "How on earth did you get way out here?"

"I don't even know where we are," said Jacob. "If you can believe it, I was on the dark side of the moon only a few minutes ago."

"No, I don't believe that," said the girl. "My dad is not going to like you being here. He doesn't like anyone trespassing."

"Where are we?" asked Jacob.

"The Secret Forest," said the girl.

"That's original," said Jacob.

The sarcastic nature of the remark was lost on the young girl, so after a few seconds of unsuccessful reasoning in her head, she moved on.

"We don't allow visitors here," she said, her face suddenly serious. "The adults say that the outside world is a terrible awful place."

"So is it terrible or awful?" asked Jacob.

"Well, both I suppose. I don't really know for myself."

"You mean that you've never been out of this forest?"

"Nope. I'm not allowed. If I left, I would be committing treason. And my father is the king so that wouldn't be such a smart move on my part."

"So you're a princess," smiled Jacob. "I thought you might be."

"How could you have thought that?" she asked.

"Well, maybe it was just the lighting," Jacob said, tilting his head to the side and squinting as if it was going to somehow convince her that he really had thought that.

"Well I *am* a princess and it doesn't matter what you think either way," she said, with confident finality.

She started to walk away, but Jacob wasn't about to let her leave him alone in the forest.

"It's a shame really," he said, with a step toward her. "At first I thought you were going to help me, but seeing as how you are a princess, I guess I can assume you are also rich and spoiled and accustomed to having everything done for you."

"I am not!" she declared. "I'm actually very nice. Just to prove it to you, I'm going to leave you in this forest all by yourself."

This was not what Jacob had wanted. He in fact was hoping for the opposite reaction.

"That is not a bit nice," he argued.

"Sure it is," she replied. "You obviously enjoy making young sensitive women feel bad about themselves for your own gratification. My mother warned me about boys that do that. So by leaving you out here and letting the harsh jungle night teach you a lesson or two, I will be saving you from your own insensitivity, and curing the population of another rude, thoughtless boy."

Jacob saw her point. He resented it when girls were smarter than him, but apart from apologizing he was out of options. He stood there looking sad for a few moments, and tried to will himself to say he was sorry. Unfortunately, Jacob had yet to learn that the terrible feeling that comes with admitting the other person is right and you are wrong is all part of the process and should be expected. As he stood there with his eyebrows tightly knit together and his hands sweating, the Princess' resolve melted at his effort.

"Well, I guess that's good enough," she said. "I can't expect all boys to be as straightforward in their feelings as a girl. Mother mentioned that as well. Come on, I'll take you to the city."

Together, they ventured into the forest, and Jacob followed the princess until she led him to a rather large city. The towers reminded Jacob of a drawing of an ancient Aztec city he saw once in a museum. The great stone structures broke forth from the thick jungle surroundings, and the stone shown in the sun as if it were plated with gold and silver. They snuck in through a small breach in the stone between two great trees that grew up over the wall. They came to a busy marketplace, all aflutter with the haggling of trade and pungent with the aroma of exotic spices and fruits. Jacob felt somehow more alive as he followed the Princess, weaving through tents dyed a deep crimson and brushing past huge swaths of fine silk hung to display their intricate patterns. Jacob almost lost the purple-ruffled dress that he was following when it disappeared up a steep staircase. The staircase led to an impossibly huge royal hall, and the Princess instructed Jacob to wait there while she went to see her father. After she had ascended another staircase up to the highest level of the palace, he had a look around.

Though from the outside, the architecture resembled that of an ancient Roman ruin come back to life, the inside of the palace was far more grandeur in nature. The spotless white marble staircase issued forth as the predominant structure in the spacious chamber. The ceiling-high columns that flanked the wide first step were embellished with birds and plants that Jacob had never seen in his life. The stunning artistry was alive with the shimmer of gold and the glint of precious gems. Jacob was so awestruck by the beauty of the structure that he failed to notice several voices nearby.

"I see that and raise you a year's worth of my best livestock!" yelled a voice from around the marble banister.

Jacob ventured over to find from whom the voice had come.

"I take that bet and raise you two of my best slaves!" another voice returned.

Jacob was surprised to discover a large poker table

covered in cards and cigars. Around it sat five or six large oddly, yet ornamentally dressed older gentlemen laughing and blowing smoke here and there. Next to each of them stood five or six smaller individuals holding cards and moving chips and tokens on and off the table.

"What are you all playing?" asked Jacob.

"What we are playing is none of your concern unless you are royalty young man, and you do not much resemble royalty, I am sorry to say," said one of the large gentlemen.

"Well, I'm friends with royalty," replied Jacob. "I met the princess just today."

"The king finally produced an heir?" asked one of the men. "That's news to my ears. Good for him. I'm glad someone around here is doing his job."

"Yes, tell him congratulations when you see him," said another.

"You must understand," began another. "We cannot really be bothered with keeping up to date with every event that occurs round here. We keep much to busy playing Hearts and Spades and Diamonds and Clubs."

"You mean poker?" asked Jacob, unable to discontinue staring at the men's obtrusive outfits.

"If I had meant poker, I would have said so," came the reply. "But since I have no idea what you are talking about, I will repeat myself so that I am completely clear."

The gentleman snapped his fingers and the man standing next him began to address Jacob in a boisterously annoying fashion.

"Let it be heard that my lord is in fact playing Hearts and Spades and Diamonds and Clubs," said the servant.

"We like to keep servants close by in case any menial tasks need to be done," said the gentleman.

The servants seemed to be busier than the gentlemen they were serving. In fact, it appeared to Jacob that they were dealing, holding the cards, taking and placing bets, and even making the crucial decisions themselves.

After a moment of attempting to follow the action on

the table Jacob made a pervasive remark. "They're just playing the game for you," he said. "You aren't even paying attention."

"It may seem that way," said one of the gentlemen, "But you should know that we are in fact performing the most important task of the game."

"What is that?" asked Jacob.

"Smoking," replied all the gentlemen in concurrence.

They each took a drink of something strong, and relit a new round of cigars.

"Don't forget that we are also doing the drinking," said another. "Also, at the end of the game, we are ones who have to pay for it all. I mean, I could lose a fortune this round and my servant couldn't care less. I'm the one who has to hand it over at the end of the day."

"Very true," said another. "We are the beneficiaries to the sport after all. All these men have to do is wait on us hand and foot while every once in a while pulling off a four of a kind or straight flush to keep us happy."

"That sounds a lot like poker to me," Jacob muttered under his breath.

"Well, it isn't," said one of the gentlemen, now taking a harsher tone toward the boy. "Who are you, anyhow?"

Jacob swallowed his tongue, yielding lest he utter another brash remark. He could see that these men would be easily upset by any perceived incivilities.

"Darnish," he politely replied.

"Perhaps this kid is royalty after all," said one of the gentlemen. "His name certainly sounds royal enough. Of course I haven't seen him around here before. Perhaps he's from the neighboring village."

"Oh! Perhaps he is," said another, joining in with overly genial looks around the table.

It seemed as if a joke had been told that Jacob somehow failed to understand. "The neighboring village?" he asked, curious to see if these gentlemen would deliver any sort of useful information on the subject. "Is it as beautiful as this place?"

"Certainly not," was the answer. "It's a dreadful ugly place."

The nods around the table seemed to confirm the tainted surmise.

"Well couldn't you do something about that?" asked Jacob. "You seem to have plenty of beauty around here to share."

"Help them!" shouted one of the gentlemen, furiously distressed with Jacob's question. "Why on earth would we do that? You obviously are not from around here if you would ever think about helping them. You see, the neighboring village is a cruel, vicious place. They don't care about anyone at all, and they show it by often attacking our beautiful city with their hoards of arrows, marching men, and battering rams."

"He's right," another affirmed. "They are terrible, terrible people. We tried to set them straight by bringing some of them over here and putting them to good work, but they are just not very reasonable. We gave them so many wonderful jobs to do, such as these fine chaps are performing right now."

He motioned to the forced servants standing around the table playing cards for their masters.

"Of course their countrymen have no sense of appreciation for our kind acts of service. They seem to fight us day and night over the issue. We don't pay much attention though, they will never be able to take a city as strong as ours."

"Well we thought as much until last week," said another. "It was a very close call."

"Ah yes a very close call indeed," was the reaction from around the table.

"But we've outsmarted them this time," said another. "You see, we were so overwhelmed with leading our armies and making battle plans that we decided to pass the job on to our servants. Ha! Imagine that! Now their own countrymen will be defending our borders against them. The neighboring village will be so outplayed."

"It was a clever move, if I say so myself," another piped in. "And now we have all the time in the world to play game after game of Hearts and Spades and Diamonds and Clubs. Don't mention it to the king though if you run into him. He's always going on about our laziness and utter lack of intelligence. Of course, he was never keen on the idea of bringing them here anyhow. It's not like he does much to help out in our efforts though. Ever since the incident, he has been so distracted."

Jacob had heard enough. He slowly backed away from the table and tiptoed to the staircase that eventually led up to the king's chamber. It was a long walk to the split in the staircase. Jacob went left only to reach the balcony and find out that he could have gotten to it going either way. Another smaller staircase led up to a long hall, and he eventually came to a pair of brass doors that were cracked open a pinch, so he quietly looked in. A deep, concerned voice issued from within.

"I just want what's best for you," said the voice. "Your mother had so many things in mind for your future. I know that sometimes I don't make the best decisions as king, but I hope that at least I can be a good father. Please don't be upset if I don't live up to your expectations as I once thought that I would. It's just not the same without the Queen around. I wish I had lost all this, and kept her instead."

"I know father," said the princess. "If mother were here, she would be proud of you. I'm not even grown up yet and I am already proud."

"You always know how to brighten me up," said the voice, now a bit more cheerful than at first.

Suddenly, the door that Jacob had been listening at flung open and a sturdy old man stood before him, dressed in robes of the same color and design as what the princess wore. He wore a wide grin, but his eyes were glistening with tears. The propinquity between father and daughter was evident, though his short gray beard and big bushy gray eyebrows that sat under a large forehead were certainly distinct. His eyes were big and brown like hers.

"I thought I heard something," said the regal man. "Who is this, Sylvia?"

"That's the boy I told you about," the princess answered. "I don't know his name though. I forgot to ask. I know that's bad manners."

"What is your name, son?" asked the man.

"D-d-darnish," gulped Jacob, guiltily. It seemed strange to Jacob that the first name that came to his mind was not his own.

"Curious name," said the man. "I am King Fredrick."

"It's good to meet you," said Jacob, his voice trembling.

"What brings you to The Secret Forest?" asked the king. "I hope you are not from the neighboring village, because you won't find very many friendly people here. Of course, you really don't look it. I do wonder how you found your way into our woods though." The king eyed Jacob curiously, yet delicately.

It's a long story," said Jacob.

At first the king had severely frightened him, but now Jacob felt quite comfortable. King Fredrick's kind voice and gentle movements even caused Jacob to forget about the formalities that should have been addressed while meeting someone of such high stature.

"Well, I would be glad to hear it over dinner," said King Fredrick, exiting the room and gesturing that Jacob and Sylvia follow him. As he strode steadily down the hall, they each walked on one side. "...If you would care to stay and join us. Sylvia is always telling me how she wishes she had more friends her age to talk to."

"I would be delighted," said Jacob, suddenly remembering to speak as formally as possible.

He was beginning to feel the hunger of not eating for half a day. Then he thought back to how good the chalky oatmeal had tasted. Then he thought about Levi and Darla being left alone in the darkness.

"Great!" said Princess Sylvia, desiring to flail her arms

in excitement yet steadfastly restraining herself. "We shall make a grand ball about it, and every kind of food is to be prepared."

"Every kind of food?" asked King Fredrick.

"Well, we don't know what Darnish likes," said the princess, tactfully.

The king laughed heartily.

"Alright, we shall have a grand meal then," he conceded.

At this moment in time, Jacob was beginning to feel that everything in life was satisfactory. He was about to share in a grand meal with a beautiful young princess and a kind and generous king. They would even ask him to stay for a while and learn about the enchanting city. He was to be treated as a guest of the highest esteem, and that sounded so delightful that he could see no way that the evening could go wrong. Of course, because I know what is going to happen, I understand that things would not turn out the way he had hoped, and if you have any sort of narrative aptitude, you should have guessed that as well. And seeing as we have both managed to reach this point, I would assume that it is safe to say that you do. So, since we both know that things cannot go as planned, we should might as well just get it over with and allow the terrible events that were to unfold happen sooner instead of later. With that being said, there came a terrified cry from the city down below.

King Fredrick strode hastily back to his chambers. Sylvia, with a look of foreboding hidden within her gentle features, turned and ran after her father. Jacob followed. The king tore open the balcony doors and searched the cityscape for the origin of the cry, spying a regiment of soldiers emerging from the forest.

"The neighbors are here!" echoed an announcement from the palace hall.

"Those blasted neighbors just don't know when to stop," said the king, stepping back inside, with a weary shake of his graying head.

Suddenly, a wayward arrow found its way over the palace walls and through the balcony window where the king stood. It pierced his shoulder from behind. Collapsing onto the bed railing, he called for his personal aid. Sylvia and Jacob ran to his side.

"Oh father!" shouted Sylvia, clutching his side.

"King Fredrick!" shouted Jacob, shocked by the horribly unexpected occurrence.

Jacob offered his shoulder for the king to lean on as he sat up against the bed. The king's personal servant and fellow countryman flew into the room, calling for the doctor.

"No!" answered the king. "There's no time. I must rally my troops."

"But sir," said the servant, "The neighbors form a middling army, I wouldn't be surprised if the guards on duty could handle the uprising themselves."

"No," said the king. "Their armies have never worked together like this before. I saw myself. They are massing too quickly at the edge of the forest. I am afraid that we are not prepared for an attack such as this. I must have time to issue a defensive strategy."

"I'm afraid there is no time for that now," came a voice from the hall.

The head of palace security leaned against the door, panting.

"The city is taken. We have a few minutes at the most before they come parading up these stairs. It is over, my lord. We just weren't ready for this. I'm…sorry," and with this he fell to his knees, his head hung in disgrace.

The king lifted himself and hobbled over to the balcony once more. Witnessing the dismantling of his beautiful city's walls and the grouping of relentless soldiers at his own doorstep, he conceded.

"Sylvia, I need you to listen to me," he began, sitting back down on the bed with a wince.

"Yes, father. What is it?"

"I need you to leave the Secret Forest."

To Sylvia, these words were devastating. Her eyes searched her father's face, wanting desperately for him to recant the words she hoped she would never hear. In her mind, it was utterly forbidden.

"No, father! I would never do such a thing! It is unforgivable."

"Sylvia, do not be stubborn. I am the King and I tell you now that you must leave. Also, I am your father and I know what's best for you. Now you must listen to me. It is the only way to keep you safe. Otherwise they may take you away from me, and I could *never* let that happen."

Sylvia crossed her arms in defiance and turned away from the king. Her face scrunched up as if she was about to throw a fit, but her father ignored it.

"Go with Darnish. He will take you away from here. But you cannot stop. You must keep going until you are completely out."

Jacob felt a sudden weight of expectation fall on his shoulders. He did not want to lead away a princess, especially with the charge of keeping her safe. Sure, in his daydreams the thought of rescuing a princess would have been 'all in a day's work,' as they say. But now, when he was faced with the real danger of a pursuing army of angry soldiers, he had no courage left to comply with the request.

"Sir," he began, trying to sound as diplomatic as possible. "I don't know the way out of the forest. I am not even exactly positive how I arrived here in the first place."

"You must take her," said King Fredrick, sternly. "I am counting on you to bring my daughter to safety. Here."

Reaching for a lever along the wall, King Fredrick revealed a passageway into a dark tunnel that opened next to his bed. There was an ever-widening dark circle around his wound, and beads of sweat were forming on his princely brow.

"Take this tunnel until you come out into a clearing. You must cross a shallow river, and then directly in front of you will be an entrance to The Caves of Remembrance."

"You cannot send them in there!" gasped the king's

servant.

"I know what I'm doing," answered the king, compellingly. "They will be fine. Sylvia, listen to me. Forget everything you have heard about those caves. All you need to remember is that you must keep running. Never stop running."

Sylvia felt horrible inside. She could not believe that her father was telling her to leave the forest or enter The Caves of Remembrance, but she trusted her father. So she attempted to show as much courage as she could bear to express.

"I will go," she said, and with a glance at his shoulder, "You will be fine without me, right father?"

"Yes, child," he said, reverting once more to a gentler, kind-hearted tone. "Remember that my love for you is always."

"My love for you is forever," she said, wrapping her arms around him tightly, sobbing deeply into his embrace.

Footsteps pounded up the great staircase down the hall from the king's quarters. The neighbors had found their way in and were storming the palace. The king's servant woke the palace guard from his stupor and exited the room, attempting to give the king as much time as they could before the soldiers would arrive.

"Go, now," the king said with finality, holding Sylvia by the shoulders, then pointing to the tunnel. "Don't hesitate, and don't turn back, no matter what you hear."

Sylvia went first, and Jacob followed her. She turned around to get one last glance at her father as he sat there. He smiled at her.

"Come on," said Jacob, turning around.

As he turned to face the long dark tunnel, all of a sudden he felt an obstructively eerie presence. His heartbeat was like a stampede of elephants. It was as if someone who should not have been there had just arrived. At first he just thought it was the emotion of witnessing such a solemn departure mixing with the adrenaline that made him sick, but then he remembered where he had last encountered the same feeling. He looked past the king, and there at the entrance to the room he saw it. Standing under the frame of the door was the black figure that he had seen in the space station. It's shadowy garments floated into the room as it eyed the king.

"King Fredrick!" shouted Jacob. "Wait!"

The figure's dark eyes (or better yet, the depression where a pair of eyes should have been) suddenly directed their attention to Jacob. Then the door to the tunnel was shut. Jacob slammed himself against the door, but it did not budge.

"Wait! We have to go back!" shouted Jacob.

"He said not to turn back," said Sylvia, wiping her tears. "We must do as he requested. We have to make it to the caves."

She took Jacob's hand and pulled him away from the door.

"You have to take me there," she said.

Jacob flushed with shame. He felt less than qualified to lead her, but the excitement of the moment was beginning to stir inside him. He looked into her wet struggling eyes and he shared a propelling grief. His chest lifted with determination.

"Okay," he said, nodding his head and gripping her hand tighter.

Chapter 4: The Caves Of Remembrance

Jacob and Sylvia hurried through the tunnel until they found themselves on a dark staircase. They descended slowly so they wouldn't lose their footings, but their steps still faltered once or twice. Eventually arriving at a stone barricade, they dug their way through and surfaced at the foot of a small glen.

"The Caves of Remembrance," said Sylvia, stretching her view across the glen.

"I see them," replied Jacob, peering in all directions for fear of being caught along the way.

He grabbed her hand once more and they dashed through the tall grass. It was only a hundred yards distance to the caves, but a small barrier of trees made them lose their way a bit. They were almost to the mouth of the cave when an arrow struck the tree in front of them.

"Get down!" whispered Jacob.

Falling into a cover of brush, Jacob and Sylvia attempted to hide themselves. A soldier from the neighboring village appeared out of the woods. Another followed closely behind.

"Blasted!" said the first soldier, removing his arrow from the tree, which stood only a leap away from where Jacob and Sylvia lay motionless.

"What sort of games are you playing now?" asked the second soldier. "We need to reroute and join with the battalion or else we are certainly going to have a deal of explaining to do about where we ran off to. What have you been shooting at?"

"I thought I saw a deer," said the first soldier suspiciously as he eyed the opening in the rock.

"We are in the middle of an invasion and you fancy chasing deer through the woods? I say you are mad. I'd be more afraid for your own hide ride now, what with us being gone so long."

He glanced up and around. Jacob caught a quick look at his face and it was a simple guess to say the man was deeply anxious about something.

"Besides, there isn't any way the poor creature went into there, at least not if he had any sense." He spoke with the tone that one only acquires when about to tell of legend, "That place is marked with a dreadful curse. I heard of a lad who ventured in there when I was a boy. His father went in after him with a rope tied round his waist and a group of comrades waiting to pull him out. Eventually the rope just went loose and neither were ever heard from again."

"Wait," the first solider whispered suddenly, turning his back to the cave. "I heard something."

Jacob looked over at Sylvia uncomfortably. He didn't know how much longer he could go without moving. Then, the soldiers were gone.

"Let's go," he murmured.

They leapt up and dashed as quietly as possible to the entrance of the cave. Jacob paused at the entrance.

Sylvia motioned for him to follow her as she stepped inside.

"W-wait," said Jacob, struggling to form his thoughts into words without sounding less than courageous. "What did that soldier mean when he said this place was cursed?"

Sylvia was trying to avoid the thought herself, because she had been raised hearing the terrible tales about the caves. However, she swallowed her fear and explained as briefly as she could manage.

"The Caves of Remembrance should rather be called The Caves of Forgetfulness because of their ability to make one forget everything he has ever known."

"You mean that's it?" asked Jacob, reassured. "You just forget everything?"

"It's a terrible thing," said Sylvia. "Countless people have tried to forge a way through the caves and have never returned. The ones that do return are said to have gone mad with the loss of their own memories."

The weight of a childhood belief hung on Sylvia's mind. She would never have dared to enter the caves except that her father had persuaded her to do so. She was set in her heart to please him, even if it meant losing her mind.

"That doesn't sound all that bad really," said Jacob, entering the cave. "I wonder if it effects children the same way."

"What makes you say that?" asked Sylvia.

"Well, we haven't been alive as long as adults, so we shouldn't have as many memories to lose. Therefore, we must lose memories at a slower rate. So as long as we can just remember one thing, we should be fine."

"And what is that?" asked Sylvia, trying to understand his reasoning.

"Twice a man did understand, but never by plan, oh never by plan," said Jacob.

"What?" Sylvia asked, now duly confused.

"It's a poem that my mom used to read to me," Jacob explained. "Its means that above all else you need to remember one thing, but in this case that one thing is that we need to remember to not stop walking no matter what."

"Do you actually think that will work?" asked Sylvia, letting hope begin to cultivate.

"I know it will. We just need to remember to keep walking," replied Jacob, reassuringly. "If we can hold onto that thought, we should be able to find a way out."

Sylvia agreed and together they ventured forward. The Caves of Remembrance were not grand and open. They were instead more like a series of tunnels and small chambers that were lit solely by the light of incandescent worms that lived along the damp ceilings and walls. The air was dense with moisture, and the worms grew scant, which made it hard to see the path at times. After a few minutes of walking, neither of them felt any different, except that Sylvia began to grow a little bored.

"Hey, you're kind of smart for a boy your age," she said, trying to make conversation.

"Why do you say that?" asked Jacob.

"Well, you had the idea that we just need to remember to keep walking. That's a pretty clever thing to come up with," she said encouragingly. "And even if I forget everything else, I'm fairly certain I can remember that one simple thing."

"I hope so," said Jacob, beginning to doubt his own plan. "I guess it does seem to be working though. So far I haven't forgotten anything that I can remember."

Sylvia laughed a high, silvery laugh that sent a pleasant shiver up Jacob's spine.

"What?" Jacob asked, fraught with curiosity.

"It just sounded funny is all," she laughed. "So, where are you from, Darnish?"

Jacob had yet to inform Sylvia of his real name.

"I'm from a city, but it isn't like your city at all."

"How is it different?"

"We don't have a king, for one thing. Instead we have things like mayors and councilmen and stuff like that."

"What do they do?"

"I don't know. What does your father do?"

"He tells people what to do and how to live all day. I think everyone looks up to him because I've never heard anyone talk bad about him."

"You really seem to love him."

"Who?" asked Sylvia.

"Your father," replied Jacob.

"Oh, yes I do indeed. I wish he was here right now."

"Well, where is he?"

"I don't know. If I did, I would tell you."

"I'm sure I wouldn't mind if you did. Where is your mother then?"

Sylvia looked puzzled at Jacob.

"Well?" she asked.

"Well, what?" asked Jacob.

"I just asked you where your mother was. Aren't you going to answer me?"

"I thought I asked you that," he replied. "Either way, my mother is at work. Sometimes she works all day and doesn't come home until it is dark outside."

"Does that bother you?"

"Does what bother me?"

Sylvia paused to think about what she had said.

"When its dark outside," she decided at last.

"Oh the darkness? No, that doesn't work all day. The light does that. The darkness comes out at night."

"That's what I thought," said Sylvia.

"Of course, the rainy days are the worst," Jacob continued. "It's like I said, the rainy days are my favorite. Do you like the rain?"

"What?" asked Sylvia.

"I asked, did you hike to Spain?" replied Jacob.

Now this sounded somewhat odd to Sylvia. She had not thought that they were speaking about Spain. In fact, she did not even know what Spain was because she had never heard of it before. Jacob happened to be thinking the same thing at that very moment. He had not thought that they were speaking about Spain, and though he had heard of Spain before, he could not think of what it was either.

"Strange girl," said Jacob.

"Yes?" Sylvia answered.

"I think it has happened."

"What has happened?" she asked.

"I don't know," he replied. "I just can't help but think that there is something I should be doing right now. Do you suppose you know what it is?"

"No, I can't say that I do," said Sylvia.

Jacob and Sylvia stopped walking and stood still for a few moments in silence. They had journeyed no short distance and were now in the very heart of the cave. If they could remember what the rest of the cave had looked like, they would have realized that the room they were now in was much wider and brighter than the previous caverns. Though both of them expressed no desire to do anything but continue standing where they were, Jacob had a slight inclination that he ought to be doing something more. He looked down the tunnel that they had come from and then down another leading out of the cavern. Then he noticed that someone else was in the cave with him. It was a young girl with beautiful big brown eyes and an excessively frilly purple dress.

"Sorry," said Jacob. "I did not see you there. I hope I didn't startle you."

"Oh heavens no," Sylvia replied. "I just hope I didn't startle you."

"No, you didn't," said Jacob.

They stood there staring at one another for a few seconds until Jacob finally had the idea that he should say something else.

"Do you have the time?" he asked.

"Time for what?" she asked in return.

"I don't know," he replied. "But I can't help but think that it's something. If only I could remember."

Just then, a chill began at the back of Jacob's neck and flittered its way down his spine until it had disappeared.

"Did you feel that?" he asked.

"Feel what?" asked Sylvia.

"I'm not sure," said Jacob, "But I feel like I've felt it somewhere before."

In saying this, Jacob turned his head back toward the direction they had come. At the entrance to the narrow tunnel from which they had entered the cavernous room stood the black figure that he had last seen in King Fredrick's chambers. In the darkness, it was difficult for Jacob to witness its full shape and form.

"What is that?" he asked the girl next to him, pointing into the darkness.

Upon looking at it, she at once stepped back in fright. "Good heavens!" she exclaimed. "What is that?"

"I don't know," answered Jacob, "But I have a feeling that I've seen it somewhere before.

Suddenly, an eerie feeling enveloped both Jacob and Sylvia. Then the creature opened its mouth, forming words that melted the air like fire on ice. It spoke slowly, laughing out a hoarse and creepy whisper.

"You know me, Jacob," it said, floating toward the two children.

"Who is Jacob?" asked Sylvia, taking a step away from the creature.

"I don't know," said Jacob, "But I don't feel very good inside right now."

"Me neither," said Sylvia.

Neither of them could keep their eyes off of the black figure as it glided toward them. It seemed as if it propelled itself along the walls and through the air with its flowing misty robes.

"You will remember me," it whispered as it neared Jacob and began to float up over him.

"Remember," said Jacob. "That is what I was trying to do. What was I trying to remember?" he asked.

"I don't know," said Sylvia, staring frightfully at the blackness that was presently surrounding them.

"I was supposed to remember to keep something, but what was it?"

"I'm not sure," said Sylvia.

"No. We were supposed to remember to do something," said Jacob.

"I don't know what you are talking about," said Sylvia.

"You must know!" shouted Jacob and he began to lose sight of Sylvia. "Because we were supposed to remember. You and I. Think, Sylvia!"

Sylvia looked into Jacob's eyes.

"What did you say?" she asked, trembling because of the cold air rushing into her lungs and stinging her eyes.

"Twice a man did understand, but never by plan, oh never by plan," he said.

"What?" she asked.

"Sylvia," Jacob repeated. "Why have we stopped walking? We need to keep walking."

Grabbing her hand, Jacob unwittingly pulled Sylvia from the clutches of the icy figure and led her out of the darkness. They walked steadily through the halls of the cave, not stopping to look left or right. Unknowingly, the darkness trailed behind them, now furious that they had left so quickly. It grasped its shadowy fingers along the rocky surfaces of the tunnel, growing closer and closer to the children with every step. After a few minutes, Jacob was able to see light splitting through a crack in the distance. The exit was near, but the darkness closed in too quickly. It latched its heartless grip around Sylvia's ankle, pulling her down. She screamed and let go of Jacob's hand.

"Please!" she yelled. "Help me!"

Jacob peered down at Sylvia. He could see her laying there, being dragged slowly into the darkness, but he could not bring himself to understand the situation. It was as if he wanted to do something for her but it would have to wait until he had accomplished the most present task in his mind. "I'm sorry, Sylvia, but we have to remember to keep walking," said Jacob.

Turning around, he followed the light until a grassy meadow was just beginning to make itself visible. Just before he stepped out of the cave, a whiff of clean, cool air rushed in and filled his lungs. He was suddenly caught up in a memory of King Fredrick staring him deeply in the face.

"I am counting on you to bring my daughter to safety," were the words which filled Jacob's mind.

A solemn dread ached in Jacob's heart and he ran back into the cave faster than his feet would carry him. He leapt into the darkness and wrapped both his arms around Sylvia. He pulled and pulled but she would not be let free. Then Jacob found himself surrounded by icy hands and the terrible touch of death. He cried out.

"Help! Anyone, please help us!"

Then the darkness was too much and he collapsed.

Chapter 5: The Kind Hunter

Jacob awoke to the sound of a fire crackling. Now, I am going to let you know right now that Jacob did not die in the cave. I am sorry if you had hoped otherwise. If you indeed are one of those readers with such cruel expectations, I will try and make this story more bearable for you by continuing to add to Jacob's formidable perils. Nonetheless, at that moment in the cave, Jacob was rescued by a kind yet altogether misunderstood hunter who happened to be passing by when he overheard Jacob calling for help. And then the next thing that Jacob knew, he was sitting in front of a roaring fire, and directly across from him was Sylvia chewing a hefty chunk of roasted elk.

"You should try some of this, Darnish. Its deliciously tangible," said Sylvia with a mouth full of meat.

"All food is tangible," replied Jacob, rubbing his head and attempting to open his eyes a bit wider.

"Not imaginary food," said Sylvia in defiance.

"She has a point," said the kind hunter.

Now Jacob had yet to notice the kind hunter sitting on the stump next to the fire. He was too busy already coming up with arguments that would instruct against Sylvia's wild ideas of describing food with words like 'tangible.' However, Jacob remembered his sense of decency.

"Hi, I'm Jac-uuhh," said Jacob, slurring off the second half of his name.

Sylvia stopped chewing and gave him a funny look as if to say, "Have you forgotten your own name?" Jacob had suddenly remembered that she still knew him as Darnish, and he decided that it would not be the best time to correct that misunderstanding.

"I mean, Darnish," he quickly stated. "My name is Darnish. How do you do?"

"Oh me, I'm fine," said the kind hunter. "I just felt kind of bad seeing you two hurting like you were. Its not every day I run into children being attacked by a strange ghostly beast."

"His name is Bradan, by the way," added Sylvia, widening her eyes while chewing off another piece of charred meat.

Jacob now got a good look at the man. His broad snout stood out at once, and it paired nicely with his even broader shoulders and sturdy build. His eyes slanted, and in them was the deepness of prolonged solitude along side a glint of kindheartedness. His hair grew long, and his beard at his chin just as long, though he had trimmed that which grew around his mouth and face. He wore an animal skin cap with two horns that twisted out of it. Thick fur and animal skins covered his body, and a great worn sword lay next to him. The clasp, which held his cloak around his neck, specifically interested Jacob.

"Where did you get that?" he asked, pointing to the small object.

"Ah this?" asked Bradan the Hunter. "I made it myself. It's a salmon swallowing a lion, carved out of wood from a white ash."

"I like it very much," said Jacob. "Why a salmon?"

"The salmon is me," said the hunter, "because I hunt what no man has dared to hunt. When I was a boy, my mother used to tell me that I could do anything that I dreamed of if I knew that it was right and worked at it with every part of my being. As I was growing up, though, she was furious about my bringing home dead animals all the time, so I eventually stopped and followed her advice about going to school and becoming learned. But when I was older, one day I went to her and said, 'Mother, hunting is in me. It's what I was born to do.' And so she said, 'My son, if hunting is what teaches you to live, then hunt.' So now that is my trade."

"Its such a romantic story," sighed Sylvia.

"That's not romantic," Jacob whined. "It has got nothing to do with romance."

"It has everything to do with romance," said Sylvia. "You just don't know what romance is because you're a boy and your brain is too small to comprehend. Of course that doesn't apply to you, Bradan."

"That's okay," said Bradan. "I was never one to talk about subjects like romance or anything like that. I wouldn't know where to start. All I've ever known is hunting, but you two probably don't care for that very much."

"What sort of game do you hunt?" asked Sylvia.

"Have you ever killed a lion?" asked Jacob.

"Once or twice," replied Bradan, "Though my heart is still set on bigger game. I want to follow in the steps of the great hunters in bringing down the deadly beasts that no other man dare fight. You know, things like werebears, sea bohemians, and dragons."

Jacob sat up as his interest peaked.

"You mean you've actually killed a dragon?" he asked.

"Well, not yet," said Bradan. "I'm actually still working on it. It's hard enough just finding one, you know."

Though he had probably hunted a great deal more than enough to impress two young children, Bradan still wanted to change the subject. He felt a fright of embarrassment at admitting that he had yet to vanquish his most formidable foe.

"Would you care for some coffee, Darnish?" he asked Jacob, "Or perhaps a strip of roasted elk? Your friend seems to find it most enjoyable. I always say there's nothing better than a fat cut of mountain elk."

Jacob accepted the offer and bit down on a thick piece of juicy meat. He had a cup of coffee to wash it down, but then realized the necessity of another leg of meat to wash down the coffee. Bradan excused himself into the woods in order to gather more firewood, and Sylvia got up and sat next to Jacob.

"What was the meaning of that poem?" she asked. "The one you told me in the cave."

"Twice a man does understand?" asked Jacob.

"Yes, what does it mean?" she asked again. "I remember you mentioning it again when we were lost in the dark of the cave."

"It's a reminder of man's reason for being alive," said Jacob. "I never understood it when I was little but it made more sense once my mom explained it to me."

Sylvia listened intently while Jacob recited the poem.

Twice a man did understand
But never by plan, oh never by plan
Both in his leaving and coming in
But between these never again

In being born, he feels the loss
Of solitude at his mother's cost
As he issues into nature's design
No past deeds yet degrade his mind

But as he grows into maturity
His mind weighs heavy with usury
To the draws of life succumbing
He finds true meaning slow coming

Until at last death takes him free
He begins to acknowledge his destiny
But too late does he find the time
To ponder life's aim and truth's divine

If only man could remember this
To live life decently, not squander it
By forgetting he strangely belittles
All the time he spends in the middle

Twice a man did understand
But never by plan, oh never by plan
Both in his leaving and coming in
But between these never again

"Those are very pretty lines," said Sylvia. "I cannot guess how you remember them all. Tell me what it means."

Jacob had not heard what Sylvia had said because he was lost in thoughts about his childhood. He remembered sitting in his mother's lap, hearing the words spoken rhythmically in her gentle voice. Sylvia drew Jacob back into the conversation by poking him several times in the side.

"Darnish, what are you thinking about?" she asked.

"Oh, nothing," said Jacob. "I was just trying to remember what it meant is all. It was in a book that my mom used to read me all the time before I went to bed. I heard it so many times it just stuck with me. I don't know what ever happened to that book. But I think the point is that everyone is here for a reason and we sometimes forget about that because of all the stuff we feel like we need to do."

"Oh," said Sylvia. "So it's sort of like when I'm supposed to be finding herbs in the forest but I get distracted by all the lovely little bugs and flowers on the path. Sometimes I think they know I'm coming and they just want attention."

"Yeah I guess it's like that," said Jacob. "I can't really think of any good examples really. I bet my mom could though."

The two children sat in silence, both wondering what the other one was thinking about. Sylvia was thinking about Jacob's mom, and then she started thinking about her own father. Jacob, being the young boy that he was, started off thinking about Bradan the Hunter slaughtering wild beasts and legendary monsters but then his thoughts dwindled away and he ended up staring into mid-air, really thinking about nothing at all.

"Darnish," began Sylvia, looking down at the ground next to her and then closing her eyes. She sighed a revealing sigh of remorse, which concerned Jacob enough that he placed his hand on her arm, trying to seem comforting.

"Yep. What is it?" he asked.

"Do you think my father is going to be alright?"

Jacob did not want to cause her any grief or need for

worry so he thought carefully about his next words.

"Yes, I think so," he said, giving her a little smile. "He seemed like a fairly clever and tough dad to me. I don't think you have anything to worry about with those neighbors and all. I'm sure your dad can handle himself just fine."

Sylvia was encouraged and she smiled back with a wide, genuine grin that glowed brighter than the blaze beside them. Fortunately for her, she believed Jacob's words much more than he had.

"Yes, I think so too," she said.

Just then, Bradan came marching back with an armful of logs while exuberantly chanting a hunting tune of his own making.

"I don't get much chance to sing out here," he said as he sat back down on the log. "It may seem like I would, but I have to be quiet to keep the animals around. They don't care too much for my singing I suppose."

"I can't see why not," said Sylvia. "I was certainly impressed. Weren't you, Darnish?"

"Oh yeah, I guess so," Jacob said.

"Darnish, tell me about that monster in the cave," said Bradan, changing the subject in no roundabout manner. "I've never met anything like that in all my years of hunting. It took all my might to pull you and Sylvia from its grasp. After I got you out of the cave, I took a shot at it with one of my arrows, but it had no effect on the beast whatsoever. It was almost as if it suddenly turned hallow and then disappeared into the darkness. I tell you, I would stay away from creatures like that in the future if I were you."

"Well, we didn't run into it on purpose, obviously," said Jacob. "I just can't seem to get away from it is all."

"You mean you've seen that thing before?" asked Sylvia. "I thought it just lived in the caves."

"No, definitely not," said Jacob. "I've actually come across it a few times before. Once I saw it while in space and the other time it was…"

Jacob stopped mid-sentence, realizing that it would be

a bad idea to bring up the fact that he had briefly witnessed the phantom-like creature lurking in King Fredrick's chambers.

"…someplace else," he said, finishing the thought. "To be honest, I think it may be following me."

Sylvia gasped and put her hands to her mouth. "Can you be serious?" she asked. "Oh Darnish, please tell me you are just telling us a tale for wicked fun."

"I'm afraid not," said Jacob. "It's true."

Bradan leaned over and rested his chin on his hand. He scratched some of his shorter whiskers and then spoke up after a moment. "It doesn't sound like any predators I've ever encountered," he said. "Perhaps there is a deeper tie of some sort. Though, I'm not much for philosophy and whatnot. I couldn't really tell you anything useful I'm afraid. The best philosophy I ever had is to just stay alert, keep my senses about me, and sleep with my eyes open. Oh yes, and to always carry a big knife."

"That does sound rather safe," said Sylvia. "I might try the first two."

"You know who might be able to help you," began Bradan. "You might go ask Simple the Wise. He's an old man that I met one time while venturing out into the wilderness. I found him up on a green hilltop, sitting peacefully. When I asked him why he was there, he told me that he had been there for over twenty years, pondering the many mysteries of the universe. When I questioned him about some of the mysteries that I have faced, his answers were full of profound wisdom. I discovered a town close by and everyone there agreed that Simple had come up with an answer for just about every question they could muster. I keep meaning to go back one day and ask him if he could solve my problem of having a lack of dragons to slay. In fact, I would *very* much like him to address that matter. I suppose I could take you there to see him if you like."

"That would be delightful," said Sylvia. "He sounds very promising. I am sure that someone like that could easily find a solution to our shadowy creature problem. I don't know if I could stand seeing that horrible monster again. It gave me such a fright, you know."

"Yes, I agree," said Jacob. "We ought to ask him."

"Then it's settled," exclaimed Bradan, beginning to gather his belongings into a satchel. "You two make sure you've had plenty to eat before we leave though. Over that hill behind us is a field, and across that field is a river that we must cross before we get to a road that will lead us to the town of Endall, which is right next to where the old man sits on the hill all day and night. We might even be there before dark if we hurry."

Bradan had been so busy with all the excitement of packing his things in anticipation of traveling with his newfound friends that he had briefly failed to follow his own set of rules for philosophical living. Now, most of the time this would have meant next to nothing, but in this case it unfortunately made a world of difference. It seems that when people are in the strict habit of taking a precaution, the event against which they safeguard almost never actually occurs. It is only when the person steps out of the ritual of preparation, even if only ever so briefly, that the event actually unfolds and they find themselves wondering why it never happened when it would have been more convenient. This was precisely the case for Bradan as he looked up from bundling together his things.

"Don't move," he said with a look of fire in his eyes.

Now, most of the time when someone says don't move, one's initial reaction is to immediately move as quickly as possible. This point would argue well for both Jacob and Sylvia's keenness; seeing as how, upon being instructed not to move, they did exactly as told.

"What's the matter?" Jacob whispered cautiously, for fear that their present circumstances had just changed dramatically.

"There are two Seahowl werebears flanked by a Greybearded dragon right behind you," said Bradan.

Now the fact that Jacob and Sylvia still did not move probably also says something about their intelligence, but I really cannot guess what that might be considering they both knew that there was no way on earth that two werebears and a dragon were right behind them. I can think of several ordinary people who, in such a situation, would have jumped up laughing about how they had believed the gimmick for a second but then had proceeded to turn around and discover that there was in fact neither a dragon nor any sort of bear in the vicinity at all. Perhaps it was Bradan's face, fashioned stern as stone, that kept them in their place.

"Is he joking?" Jacob gasped to Sylvia. "I can't tell. Bradan, are you serious?"

"Oh, yes," said Bradan with a madly passionate grin slowly growing on his grim face. "I'm serious all right. Though this is a bit odd considering Greybearded dragons have a particular preference for Seahowl werebears. Now I want you two to slowly get up and walk toward me. Not too fast though. We don't want to spook them, and we especially don't want to entice them. Well, not yet anyway." He ended this somewhat disconcerting speech with a low, throaty laugh.

Jacob and Sylvia moved toward Bradan, and as they did so they peered behind them. This was the moment when they realized that approaching were in fact two werebears and a dragon exactly as Bradan had said. The dragon was about forty feet in length and twenty feet tall at the shoulder. It had acid yellow and ruby red scales that nearly blinded Jacob and Sylvia with the burst of reflecting sunlight. Its eyes were black and dead like shark's eyes. The werebears were not nearly as towering, but their wicked faces inflicted a greater degree of terror upon Jacob and Sylvia's mind. Huge fangs erupted from their long, snarling snouts. Their eyes, unlike the dragon's, were rolling around in their skulls, alive with fury. Their fur looked thick and sharp, as if the skin was covered in small quills. From where he stood, Jacob could see that their paws contained short, cruel claws. They approached their prey slowly. The dragon crept behind them toward the three friends next to the fire, agile as a housecat.

"You must leave at once," said Bradan to the two children who now stood next to him. "Quickly, run up the hill and escape across the field. Once you cross the river, you should be safe."

"No," said Jacob, acknowledging the peril Bradan was placing upon himself. "We cannot just let you hold them off while we get free. There has to be another way."

"I don't intend to hold them off," answered Bradan, now burning with the emotion of the hunt. "I intend to kill them. Now go quickly, I must know that you two are safe." The air around them crackled with the kinetic energy of the inevitable fight.

"Let's do as he says," said Sylvia, taking Jacob by the arm. "Bradan is right. There isn't anything we can possibly do."

Jacob stayed in his place for a few moments, sweating over what was about to occur. He did not want to leave but he knew that he really had no choice.

"Alright, let's go," he said, following Sylvia up the hill and into a grouping of small trees.

They stopped on the edge of a ridge that overlooked the valley. Bradan was nearing the beasts, sword drawn and ready. He walked as one who wielded great power, preparing for a sudden reckoning of strength and skill. The two werebears circled around him as the dragon went in for the first strike. It thrust its jaws toward his sword-wielding arm, biting the air as he dodged its attack. He gave it a swift blow to the cheek with his fist and it jerked sideways, throwing him into the air. Bradan caught hold of a hanging branch and swung down on top of a werebear. The shock caused it to stumble about, attempting to shake its foe to the ground. Bradan tore into its spiny back with the sword. The other werebear released its kin from the grip of Bradan's blade by charging around to one side and biting fiercely into the warrior's leg with its fangs. Bradan fell into the dirt and was drawn across the ground. The werebear shook him from side to side and then the dragon took hold of his shoulder. They each pulled him in opposite directions, stringing him up in the air.

"Oh no!" screamed Sylvia, clinging to Jacob's arm while witnessing the event.

"He can do it," said Jacob, nudging her to continue up the hill. "He's got to."

Then Jacob looked and saw that there was another beast in the ravine. This one however was moving fast like the wind. It tore through the trees, gathering darkness to itself. It was a visceral sight, watching the coal-like dark overtake the green of the forest. The day did not seem so bright and cheery as it had only moments before.

"It's the shadowy figure from the cave," said Jacob, gasping. "It's headed for Bradan."

"We have to do something," shouted Sylvia, now struggling to keep herself from crying. "Please, Darnish! Help him!"

"Sylvia, we must run now," Jacob said, his voice becoming quite and stern. He pointed down into the ravine. "Bradan can handle himself."

About fifty feet down the hill was a third werebear that had just come into view out of the forest. It was headed straight for Jacob and Sylvia, eyeing the two children with a devilish hunger. Its face resembled that of a bear, but it also elongated slightly into the shape of a large wolf, which seemed to drool through the sharp protrusion of monstrous teeth curving from its panting mouth.

"Jacob!" Sylvia gulped, being overcome with trepidation.

"Run," said Jacob, taking her hand and pulling her view away from the bear.

The last sight that Jacob caught of Bradan caused his heart to ache. The werebears were tearing into his skin as the dragon blew fire across his body, and at the last moment, the dark figure enveloped him in shadow.

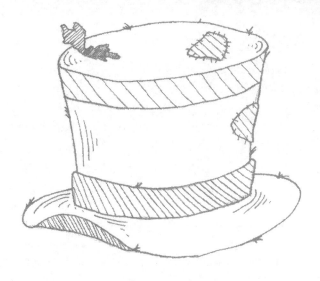

Chapter 6: A Stranger In The Woods

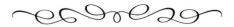

Jacob and Sylvia dashed away, leaping quickly over roots and foliage, ever keeping their eyes on the field in front of them. As they came out into the clearing, they knew that this would be the most dangerous part of their escape. It was a straight sprint through the grass. They were about half way across the field when the werebear stepped out into the sunlight. Because of the distance they had set between it and themselves, the werebear suddenly took off in a dead sprint of pursuit. Jacob looked back, fearfully noticing that it was gaining on them drastically with every bound.

Now, I know what you might think a ferocious werebear would do to two children Jacob and Sylvia's size, but I don't really want you to think about that at the moment because that might put a damper on this whole story. I would guess that most people don't want to read a tale, however clever it may be, that involves two children being mauled by a bear. It's just not a very inviting subject. However, the story would not be nearly as interesting if the two children were never given the chance to be mauled and eaten at all. Because of that fact, I've decided to make a compromise. I feel that I should let you know right now that the bear does end up eating one of them.

So now I am going to give you a chance to swallow that fact because I know that it is an overall terrifying idea indeed. And while you ponder the intricacies of a story's moral obligation to protect the reader's delicate emotional state, I will remind you that stories have no obligation to do anything of the sort. In fact, the story cares little about what you think whatsoever. That is just the way it is, and there is no changing it. It is often said that "These things don't write themselves," but I beg to differ. If I recorded the story any different than it actually occurred, it would cease to be the story in question and would actually become a completely different story altogether. So now that I have rambled on long enough for you to accept the reality that one of the children is going to be eaten, I will continue with the adventure.

Jacob did not stop running, but instead he kept telling his legs to go faster and faster. Surprisingly, Sylvia stayed up with him, even in her distressed state. In a familiar forest, Sylvia would have been pronounced the faster of the two, but at an open sprint Jacob held the lead. They had just reached the edge of the grove of trees that followed the riverbank when Jacob realized that there was no way that they would be able to make it to the river before being overtaken by the werebear. Due to this sudden understanding of their current plight, he made an executive decision.

"Hurry, Sylvia. We'll climb a tree," he shouted as he ran.

Choosing the first large tree in their path, Jacob leapt up onto a thick branch and helped pull Sylvia up behind him. They climbed higher and higher, hoping that the bear would pass by or give up the search, but the werebear was soon beneath them, climbing up onto the first branch.

"He's coming up after us," said Sylvia, placing little hope in their elevated state.

However, just as she made this remark, the limb on which the bear had rested its weight snapped and it fell to the ground, startled. It was large, even for a werebear, and the branches would not be able to hold such a mass. Resolutely, it then attempted to climb straight up the trunk, but it once more failed and went crashing down. Jacob and Sylvia breathed a sigh of relief as it circled the bottom of the tree, clawing impatiently at the bark. Eventually, with a sniff of disgust, it turned itself around and paced away.

"I think that's done it," said Jacob. "Now we just wait until it's completely out of sight and then we cross the river."

"I thought it was going to catch us there for a little bit," said Sylvia. "I don't think I've ever seen anything so fierce in my life. All I could imagine as I ran was that horrible beast gobbling me up."

She wrapped both of her arms around herself as if someone she loved was giving her a hug of assurance.

"Well, I don't think you need to worry about that now," said Jacob. "And if it makes you feel any better, we can stay up in this tree as long as you want."

Unfortunately for Sylvia, Jacob was wrong in suggesting that she had nothing to worry about. Because, if you remember from a few paragraphs earlier, I did mention that one of the children is going to be eaten. Sylvia, however, was now even unaware of a lingering possibility that such an event might happen.

"I wish I was a bird," she said, turning her thoughts to happy imaginings.

Jacob laughed a hearty laugh, mostly to relieve his own fearfulness.

"Why do you say that?" he asked.

"Because then I could stay up in the trees forever," she replied. "And I wouldn't have to leave the forest ever. I shall grow ever so homesick if I am away from it for too long. My mother always said, 'God put the forest there for humans to enjoy, but they neglected it, so now that's where he goes when he wants to get away from people.' And my father doesn't mind me going into the forest alone. He seems to think it's safer than me being out in the city all by myself."

"That's a funny thought," said Jacob. "I guess I never spend much time outside really. I usually just spend most of my time in my room at home, or in the kitchen if my mom's cooking dinner." For a second Jacob imagined his home with all its furnishings and luxuries. Then he thought about the forest in which he had met Sylvia. A contrast of ideas floated around in his mind, and for some reason it made him feel sad, though he was not old enough to understand why.

"You love your mom, don't you Jacob?" asked Sylvia.

"Yes, I do," he said. "Why do you ask that?"

"I was just making sure," said Sylvia. "Some people don't have a mother to love, and they would be very upset if those who had a mother didn't take the time to love them."

Jacob stared off into the distance, thinking about his mom. If given the chance, he would have spent a good few minutes reciting to Sylvia some of the wonderful reasons that he loved his mother, but the opportunity was not to present itself, for Jacob shortly noticed that something was moving quickly through the forest toward the two of them.

"Sylvia, it's coming back," shouted Jacob, feeling similar to the way a child at school feels when a terrorizing bully refuses to leave them alone.

Sure enough, the werebear had backed up in order to pick up speed and it was now headed straight for the trunk of the tree.

"Hold on," said Jacob, wrapping his arms around a branch.

The bear rammed the trunk with its shoulder and the tree shook as if it were being tossed by a gale wind. Jacob maintained a firm grip, but Sylvia did not have such a good hold around the trunk and she was shaken lose. Jacob instinctively reached out to grab her but he missed, and she went tumbling head over heals downward.

"Sylvia!" Jacob shouted as she screamed all the way down.

She luckily managed to be thrown far enough that she missed any outgrowing branches. Unfortunately though, the werebear was very aware of her sudden descent and he set his bearings in order to take full advantage of the situation. As she came to the point in her drop where she would have landed flat in the dirt, the welcoming jaws of a hungry werebear instead greeted Sylvia. The bear was so large, that it easily swallowed her up in one grand motion.

"No!" Jacob quaked, shaking with a sudden rush of fright and remorse for his poor friend Sylvia.

The werebear finished gawking over his unexpected triumph and proceeded to turn his attentions to the other child who still sat in the tree, deciding how he might procure a second course.

Now, I know that witnessing a child so innocent and sweet as Sylvia being eaten by a werebear would be a horrible thing, even if one were only reading about such an experience. That is why I warned you about it before hand, so that it would not come as too great a shock when it occurred. But now that you know how kind I can be in warning you about such an event, you might have guessed that I am also too kind to let the little girl stay dead. This however, is not true. Once a character dies, they die for good. That is just something that I believe should always be the case, at least at the moment. However, it is a fortunate thing (for the valiantly kindhearted readers that is) that Sylvia is not yet dead.

Jacob did not know this, but he still gathered his courage together and began to climb down the tree in order to save his already eaten friend from the werebear. The only thought that crossed his mind at that moment was that he was about to be eaten as well and that it did not matter very much considering he had failed to protect the girl whom he had promised to protect. Just before he reached a height he deemed safe enough to leap onto the bear and attack it in a desperate frenzy, he heard an approaching whistler, who's voice delivered the most curious of tunes.

Jacob looked up to observe a very large, oddly dressed man hiking through the woods and whistling to himself a tune that for some reason sounded as if it were coming from several different voices in several different directions. At first, Jacob noticed the pale blue top hat which sat delicately on the man's head. Then he noticed the torn suit, which adorned the rest of the man's lengthy body. The man walked right up past the werebear and kept on going. Jacob thought it only appropriate to warn the man of the danger he had obviously failed to notice.

"Sir, look out! There's a werebear!" shouted Jacob.

"Woah, who said that?" asked the man, spinning round and round while holding onto his hat, trying to find the direction from whence the voice had come.

"I did," said Jacob, sternly. "You must climb that tree quickly or else that werebear may eat you. It just ate my only friend. I'm telling you; it may eat you as well."

"What werebear? Oh, that werebear," said the man, now noticing the bear which stood a few feet in front of him.

The bear had taken no notice of the man up to that point, but it instead kept its attentions on Jacob. Jacob began to cry. The emotions that follow losing one's only friend suddenly caught up with the boy and he was overwhelmed with sorrow. The man noticed his weeping and felt sorry for the crying boy in the tree.

"What is the matter?" asked the man, walking closer to Jacob and standing next to the bear. "This bear isn't giving you any trouble is it?"

"It ate my only friend," Jacob cried.

"Aw, I see," said the man, pausing to think about someone long ago who he had lost. "Well, how long ago was that?" he perked up.

"Just a minute ago perhaps," said Jacob.

"Only a minute ago?" asked the man, glancing at his pocket watch. "Well that isn't so bad at all then. Do you think your friend is still in one piece?"

"I couldn't say," said Jacob. "I don't want to think about it."

"Well, yes. I suppose that makes sense," said the man. "Well there is only one thing to do in a situation like this. You've got to give the bear an upset stomach."

"Why?" asked Jacob. "What good will that do?"

"Was your friend a very disagreeable person?" asked the man.

"No, she was very agreeable," said Jacob.

"Well that's no good," said the man. "Nonetheless, I will give this a try. We may just get lucky."

The next thing that the man did was not something that Jacob (nor anyone else in a similar situation) could have ever expected. He began to forcefully tickle the werebear on the underside of its belly, which caused it to roll over onto its back in a spell of werebear laughter. Jacob watched as the man tickled the bear harder and harder until it had laughed so hard and its stomach grew so upset that it vomited its breakfast all over the ground around itself. The werebear, unhappy about the current situation, got up and went off to find a drink of water, and Sylvia was left sitting in a gooey mess. Jacob climbed out of the tree and stumbled to her side.

"Sylvia?" he said.

"Yes," she replied.

"You're alive!"

"Yes, and very dirty at that," she replied.

"That's nothing a good bath in cool, clean riverwater won't fix," said the man, offering his hand to Sylvia. He had soon led the two of them to the bank of the river where Sylvia was able to clean off the horrible stink of werebear insides.

"But how on earth did you manage to get me out?" she asked, still dazed at the fact that she had escaped from such an awful and malodorous end.

"He did it," said Jacob, pointing to the man in the torn suit and blue top hat.

Sylvia looked up at the man. His face was very kind and handsome, and he reminded her of the paintings of her father from his younger years.

"It is a pleasure to meet you, sir," said Sylvia, remembering her courtly manners. "I'm Sylvia and this is Darnish."

"And you as well, young lady," said the man. "My name is Dawson Quinn, but most of my friends used to just call me Dawson."

"Well that is a wonderful name," said Sylvia. "May I add it to my List of Wonderful Names in my diary?"

"You certainly may, Sylvia," said Dawson.

"What I don't understand," interrupted Jacob, "Is how you were able to avoid being eaten by that bear yourself." Jacob, though genuinely appreciative for Sylvia's rescue, had developed a bit of resentfulness toward Dawson. One cannot fully understand why Jacob refused to express a lighter method of conduct toward the stranger (considering the circumstances), but a sensible theory is that he was simply upset that someone else had done what he had failed to do.

"Yes, please tell us how you did it," Sylvia insisted. "And how did you happen upon us?"

"Well, I was flying about next to the river," began the man.

"You were flying?" Jacob disbelievingly asked.

"Yes," said the man, not taking a second thought at Jacob's disapproving tone. "Anyway, I was flying about when I heard someone screaming. So I decided to touch down and have a little look around the woods. When I found you sitting there, Jacob…"

"You mean Darnish," Sylvia quickly corrected Dawson.

"Ah yes, I meant Darnish. Sometimes I get people's names confused. Forgive me. Anyhow, when I found Darnish sitting there and was made aware of his plight, I remembered the best way to get werebears to vomit recently eaten children was to tickle them until they coughed up the said victim. And seeing as how the werebear could not see me, it was rather easy to do."

"That is such a great story," said Sylvia.

"I suppose so," said Jacob, trying to mask his indignance in front of Sylvia. "I still don't understand why the bear didn't gobble you up. And how come you knew how to do that anyhow?"

"Like I said, the bear could not see me," said Dawson. "What is the proper term? Ah, yes. Invisible."

"Are you serious?" asked Sylvia. "You can turn invisible?"

"No, he is not serious," said Jacob, now giving Sylvia an unnecessarily disheartening glance. "Don't you know when someone is just pulling your leg?"

Dawson Quinn seemed suddenly offended at Jacob's statement and in his agitation he proceeded to hastily disappear into a whiff of cloud that quickly vanished into the wind, leaving Jacob and Sylvia alone on the outskirts of the dense forest.

"He's…gone!" Jacob shouted, taking a step back in astonishment.

"Well look, now you've made him leave," said Sylvia, disappointed that her new friend had so soon departed.

"Well, I didn't think he could actually disappear," said Jacob, now slightly embarrassed at what he had just been saying.

At Sylvia's suggestion, Jacob tried apologizing to the air several times, but to no avail. They sat and waited on the riverbank for about half an hour, but Dawson did not return.

"I guess we should be off then," said Jacob, finally.

"I guess so," Sylvia agreed, looking one final time up and down the riverbank for any sign of her rescuer.

"Hey, I'm sorry about making Dawson leave," Jacob apologized, offering his hand to Sylvia. "I am just not that used to having people disappear on me like that. I feel terrible about it now."

"It's okay," said Sylvia, sighing. "As long as I have you to travel with, Darnish, I shall be just fine."

The two friends began to stroll down the bank of the river, looking for a shallow place to cross. Jacob thought about

Dawson calling him by his real name. He thought perhaps it had been a coincidental slip of the tongue, but he could not be sure. Jacob now wished that Sylvia did in fact know him by his actual name, but he felt that to tell her now after he had lied about it would cause her to distrust him. As they walked along, his insides rumbled with thought.

Chapter 7: The Wise Man on the Hill

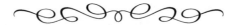

After a short while, Jacob and Sylvia came to a small bridge and I could describe to you how they crossed over it and then tracked down a long straight road and eventually came to a town, but nothing very exciting happened during that period of time, so I am going to just leave it out.

Eventually however, they did reach a town, and upon entering it, Jacob and Sylvia both began to realize that there was no one anywhere in sight. A wooden post in the town square held a sign that read 'Travelers, welcome to the town of Endall.'

Neat little wooden homes and shops lined the cobblestone streets, creating in Jacob a feeling that he had suddenly found himself in a miniature village built for a Renaissance fair. Above the shops hung carved wooden signs suspended from iron chains, and the noise of the chains swinging lightly in the wind was all that could be heard by the two curious children.

"Well, that is odd," said Jacob. "The stores seem to be open and the shops have their lamps lit, but I don't see any sign of people."

"I was starting to think the same thing," said Sylvia. "Perhaps everyone is napping at the moment. Mother used to make me nap twice a day or else I would not be allowed to venture outside in the evening."

"I don't think so," Jacob replied. "I think something *else* is going on here."

The children noticed a distinct pattern in the cobblestone that led to the center of town. At that spot, a hefty telescope had been constructed upon an iron stand.

"What do you suppose this is used for?" asked Sylvia, looking through the eyepiece at one end of the telescope.

"Perhaps it's just a monument," said Jacob, taking his own peek through the gigantic spyglass. "Actually, it seems to be in good working condition. Maybe it's for community star gazing, if people do such a thing."

Jacob swung the grand telescope across the landscape until something caught his eye.

"I think I found our wise man," said Jacob. "Look!"

Sylvia peered through and saw an elderly man sitting peacefully on the very top of a grassy knoll. The grass waved around him where he sat, still as a statue. The two children ran as fast as they could down the street and straight out of town until they came upon the hill. It was a short climb and they soon arrived in front of a tranquil, elderly gentleman wearing a russet cap and thick velvet suspenders. It should have been difficult for them to believe that they had come across the man so easily and coincidentally, but let me remind you that children are often less inclined to notice a coincidence and more inclined to assume things easy. As they came nearer to the gentleman, his face was so motionless that Jacob doubted he was alive.

"Are you Simple the Wise?" asked Jacob, leaning over to catch his breath.

The man startled with a small shudder and unassumingly looked the children up and down. Then his face showed that he was somewhat surprised to see them. He looked pensively out across the hilly landscape and replied to the question, speaking in a soft and leisurely manner.

"Though the truth is often disguised, one is either simple or wise," he said. "But not both simultaneously."

"I asked if you *are* Simple the Wise, as in your name is Simple," Jacob corrected, assuming that the man had misunderstood the question. "We heard that there was an old wise man here named Simple who had an answer for every question."

"Ah, you mean Simplé," said the man. "The accent is absolutely crucial. If you forget it, it might sound like you are calling me simple, and that would be a tragedy considering the great degree to which I am *not*."

"Well, Simplé," began Sylvia, who had been well versed in cultural pronunciation during her studies, "We would like to ask you a few questions." She then politely sat cross-legged in the soft grass of the hilltop. Jacob quickly repeated her action. He remarked to himself how much they looked like young students of a wise, old scholar in one of his favorite martial arts movies.

"I would like to ask many people many questions, but that does not change the fact that I never will have the opportunity," Simplé replied. "If there is one resource that this universe produces without fail, it is questions."

"Okay, but we are here now and we are wanting to ask you questions, so will you answer them?" asked Jacob, trying to enunciate his words as clearly as possible.

"Whether or not I answer them depends on many factors," Simplé replied; his visage, so stony a few moments ago, began to brighten, and his voice sparkled with intensity. "Have you considered that we might all perish by a great flood before you have finished your next sentence?" His mouth widened to a self-satisfied smile.

"Well, no," said Jacob. "But that doesn't seem very

likely. Anyhow, me and Sylvia have come a long way to ask you something very important."

"Importance is assigned by each person to a separate degree; what you might call one, I might call three." said Simplé. "What you consider important, I might consider rubbish."

"You certainly *consider* a lot of things," said Sylvia, finding the man's answers quaint but amusing. "But how can we be sure that you know what you are talking about?"

"I have lived," said Simplé, confidently. "Life is a teacher, of which I am only a pupil, and a deliberate pupil at that. I have made it my ambition to seek the greatest amount of wisdom possible."

"And have you found it?" Sylvia asked.

"Wisdom is not something that can be obtained, only decidedly sought," replied Simplé.

"I think wisdom can be obtained," Jacob injected, growing weary of the old man's confusing rhetoric. "At least somewhat," he added.

"How would you know?" asked Simplé. "How old are you, boy?"

"How old do I look?" asked Jacob.

"About twelve to fourteen," said Simplé, approaching an air of disdain as he spoke.

"That's a fairly good guess," answered Jacob.

I realize that I still have not yet given you Jacob's age and I know that it would be a good fact to know considering the challenges that he has faced, but I will remind you once more that he is just at that age where a young boy begins to like girls and yet still does not admit it. I would also say that this stage comes at slightly different ages for slightly different boys.

"How old are *you*?" Sylvia asked Simplé in retort.

"My age is unimportant," said Simplé. "For age does not measure one's level of learning, but being learned measures one's level of learning."

"That is stupid," said Sylvia, her tone becoming

anxious. "You just said the same thing twice. Saying a word twice does not give it any more meaning than it had the first time you said it, at least, not in this situation. Now, if my mother said a word twice, she always meant it a lot more the second time."

"Sylvia, don't be rude," said Jacob, giving her a slight nudge. He also began to doubt that the guru was all they had hoped him to be, but he was not prepared to offend the elderly man.

"Well, he is being an idiot," said Sylvia.

"You are rash, child," said the old man. "I seek to hone my ways while I am old, but I would be in no position to do so if I had not first chosen to change them while I was young. You need to amend your ways if you want to ever find the path to wisdom in this life."

"Listen sir, that's all fine and dandy, but I really have a few things that I was hoping you could help me find the answer to," Sylvia finished hopefully.

"Answers only ever lead to more questions," said Simplé.

"What is that supposed to mean?" Sylvia asked, now raising her voice and making it clear that she was irritated. "Let's go, Darnish. This guy is obviously not so very wise after all."

"The young are called wise through teeth that spread lies," said Simplé.

Sylvia had had enough. She stood up out of her sitting position, brushed off her frills, and began to march back down the side of the hill, crossing her arms and scowling as she went.

"Sylvia, hang on a minute," entreated Jacob, chasing after her. "Why are you getting so upset? We need his help." Though he did not show it, Jacob did understand very well how she felt.

"I'm angry because he is just plain impertinent," Sylvia explained. "Mr. *Simple* has not said one useful thing since we arrived. He just keeps babbling about stuff that sounds smart but really is just completely absurd."

"You're right," said Jacob. "I realize that he isn't as smart as all that, but he seems to be the only person around here, so I think we should try one more time."

"What does that mean?" Sylvia asked, changing the subject. "What do you mean by *as smart as all that*?"

"It's just a phrase I heard one time," said Jacob. "I think it means he isn't very smart, really. We ought to try once more though. He is bound to know something."

"Maybe, but it's impossible to get him to say anything practical," argued Sylvia, giving Jacob a sidelong glance. Her scowl softened at the look of his earnest face.

"Perhaps, but I've got an idea," said Jacob, turning back around. "Give me a moment."

Sylvia couldn't leave without Jacob, so she waited and watched as he walked back up the hill and past the old man. Jacob sat himself down on a hilltop that happened to be situated just a few feet higher than the one on which Simplé rested. Simplé peered over his shoulder at Jacob with a look of consternation.

"What are you doing?" he asked, with a sudden sharpness to his voice.

"I'm becoming wise," Jacob answered.

The man huffed to himself and turned back around in an attempt to remain in a state of peace, but something was clearly bothering him. After a few moments, he stood up and walked past Jacob and sat himself down on a hilltop only a slight degree higher than Jacob's. Jacob returned the notion by getting up and finding an even higher hilltop on which to become wise. Simplé repeated his rejoinder and soon found a higher ground on which he could perch in peace. This pattern persisted until both of them realized that there was one hilltop that loomed far above the rest, and a race to claim its peak suddenly erupted. They ran side-by-side, breathing forcefully and trying not to trip until at last Jacob, being far younger, arrived first and claimed his spot. Sitting down, he announced that he had won.

"It matters not who sits the higher, when even the highest can be proven a liar," said Simplé.

"Ah, but it apparently does matter," said Jacob, attempting to take the same tone in which Simplé had been speaking with them. "Your actions have told me what your words would not. If you had stayed where you were and had still been at peace, then maybe I would have believed that you hold some sort of higher intelligence, but seeing as how you desired this spot proves that you are no better than anyone else, and that you have no answers for us."

Simplé was furious. In his anger, he stomped around in circles and threw his satchel into the air. It seemed that he was not accustomed to venting, and so his tantrum appeared somewhat ridiculous to Jacob and Sylvia. Oddly however, as he danced around in a state of resentment, his form began to change. His face began to grow younger and younger and he seemed to quickly lose half of his height.

Jacob watched in shock at the transformation. He felt strangely accountable for the man's unexpected loss in age.

"Don't feel too bad," said Jacob. "You can have this spot if you really want it so much."

"Really?" asked Simplé, trying to sound grateful. His voice had changed and was becoming more childish by the second. His wrinkled face smoothed out until his cheeks were shiny and rosy as a baby's, and his body was shrinking all the while. In fact, he had changed completely into a child, and he appeared to be a few years younger than Jacob or Sylvia. Jacob, noting the strangeness of the sudden transformation, ignored it as best he could.

"All I need is for you to answer a few questions for me, and I shall give you this spot," said Jacob.

"I'll do the best I can," said young Simplé, humbly.

"First, what happened to all the people who live in Endall?" he asked.

"They all heard about an approaching flood that was surely coming to wipe them away, so they fled," said young Simplé.

"A flood?" asked Sylvia, who had just arrived at the top of the hill. She gave Jacob a surprised glance as she realized the change that had occurred in Simplé.

"Yes, they came and warned me about it, but I didn't believe them, so I stayed here. And so far nothing has happened."

"Oh," said Jacob, in relief. "Well, the next question I have is about a dark creature that has been chasing me."

"It's a terrible beast," piped Sylvia, now noticing exactly how much shorter and younger Simplé appeared. She eyed Jacob to see if he had anything to say about the matter, but he was too busy awaiting a response to his question.

"It moves like a shadow, and it has dark misty robes and a black core, and in its presence one loses all hope and is left feeling completely despondent," Jacob explained.

"Hmm," said young Simplé. "I know what you are talking about. It's on the tip of my tongue. I just can't spit it out. Perhaps if I were sitting where you currently sit, I would be able to remember."

"Oh, certainly," said Jacob, giving up his spot on the highest hilltop.

Young Simplé sat down and made himself comfortable. As he closed his eyes, he slowly morphed back into his older form.

"Now, what was I talking about?" he asked himself in his regular tone and voice. "Ah, yes the creature of shadow. I do know what that is," he said.

Jacob and Sylvia listened eagerly as Simplé cleared his throat.

"That is the creature called Destiny," he continued.

"Destiny?" asked Jacob. "Destiny is an idea, an end, or a calling. Its not a creature."

"It is a creature," said Simplé. "Some would call it a monster. Others have spoken of it as a beast from hell."

"But why is it chasing me?" asked Jacob.

"It has its reasons," said Simplé. "But I must ask," he continued, leaning over and speaking softly as if to keep the nature of the conversation from being heard. "Has it tried to kill you?"

"Yes," said Sylvia. "It tried to kill both of us. The good hunter named Bradan saved us from it."

Simplé regained his composure and sighed. "Then you will not survive," he hastily stated. "Good hunter or no good hunter, you will not be able to stand up against Destiny for very long."

"That cannot be the case," said Jacob, leaning in face-to-face with Simplé and whispering. "I told King Fredrick that I would protect his daughter and that is what I intend to do. There must be some way to stop it."

"I know of no way," said Simplé, with regret, "I am sorry."

Jacob and Sylvia were downtrodden. They felt an air of hopelessness fill their hearts. Though Simplé obviously had some issues to work out, he did seem to know what he was talking about after all. If *he* did not know how to stop the creature, then perhaps no one would. They said farewell and began to walk down the hill once more, but then Simplé called out to them.

"I just remembered," he yelled. "You should ask that question where the The Five Angels take their tea. Perhaps there you will find an answer. Just follow the signs."

"Thank you," Jacob shouted in response.

"That was so odd," said Sylvia, as they continued down into the town.

"What?" asked Jacob.

"For a few moments, I thought he appeared more like a little child than an old man. Did you notice?"

"Yes, I did. Perhaps some people only act as old as they see themselves," said Jacob, "In Simplé's case, I would say he is only as wise as he assumes himself."

Even though they were children, they both understood the importance of this revelatory statement.

"I hope we don't meet him again," said Sylvia. "It took forever just to get a *simple* answer out of him." Their eyes met and they laughed together.

"And a simple answer is all we needed," Jacob said with a final chuckle, coming up to where the telescope was mounted in the cobblestone.

Jacob looked through it once more as Sylvia read over a sign that stood a few feet away. On a pole were several dozen signs with different names on them, and each pointed in a different direction.

"I found it," said Sylvia. "This one reads, 'The Five Angels.' That is what we want, is it not?"

Jacob had been busy looking into the telescope, but now he looked back over at Sylvia with a sickened grimace. He pointed to the eyepiece. Sylvia quickly rushed over and peered inside. It was still pointed toward where the old man had been sitting on the hill. He had wandered back to his former position atop the original hill. As she looked, Sylvia could see the creature Destiny hovering over Simplé, looking as if it was about to swallow him whole. What was more evident than that however, was the massive wall of water on the horizon, peaking like a wave, and flowing at an alarming rate directly toward the town of Endall.

"It's Destiny, Darnish," whimpered Sylvia.

"I know," said Jacob. "I'd say we need to worry more about that enormous flood at the moment though. Which way did you say 'The Five Angels' were?"

"That way," said Sylvia, pointing down a narrow road that led out of town.

"We've got to run for it," said Jacob with intent.

"Again?" Sylvia said, exasperated at the thought. She gathering her skirt in her arms and prepared herself.

"It's our only chance," he said.

The two children took off running swiftly down the straight dirt road. Unfortunately, the water moved at a much hastier pace than they, and it was soon upon them.

"We've got no where to go!" Sylvia said between gasps. "It will cover us at any second."

Jacob glimpsed behind and realized that she was right.

A hundred foot wall of water spread across the landscape behind them, the peaks whitening as they turned towards the children. It looked to Jacob as if it washed in their direction with a mind specifically bent for their destruction.

"What's that?" Sylvia asked, pointing toward a train that was just picking up speed on a track that ran parallel to and only a few yards away from the road.

"A train!" Jacob shouted incredulously. "Hurry, we've got to reach the railing of the last car!"

They changed their course and were soon running up behind the caboose. Jacob was able to grab the iron railing along the backside, but Sylvia fell behind. Though she ran and ran, the train seemed to get further and further away until she had fallen about ten steps behind. Jacob stood on the balcony and reached for her, but she was too far away.

"I can't catch up," shouted Sylvia, she slowed, trying to catch her breath. "Darnish, just go without me."

Jacob opened the door to the caboose and ran through it and then through the luggage car. Upon finding a cord labeled 'Emergency Stop,' he pulled it with all his might and the train flew to a sudden halt, throwing boxes and people in the expected direction. He ran back to the back of the caboose, where Sylvia joined him.

"Well, now we have no way of escaping it," she said, looking back at the wall of angry water.

"Actually," said Jacob. "For every action there is an equal and opposite reaction. I learned that in school. So if there is an "Emergency Stop' cord, then there has to be an equal and opposite cord."

This sounded reliable to Sylvia so they ran back through the caboose and luggage cars and into the closest passenger car. Hanging beneath the 'Emergency Stop' cord was another, suitably labeled 'Emergency Go.'

"I guess that is a solid theory," admitted Sylvia, reaching out and pulling the cord.

Almost immediately, the train regained its momentum, throwing boxes and people in the other direction this time. When Jacob looked around, he realized that they were in one of the lounge cars, and it seemed as if the lounging passengers were not too happy about being tossed back and forth so often. He decided to find a place to hide.

"Here's the perfect spot," said Jacob, pointing to an empty cabin in the next car over.

"How do you know?" Sylvia asked, her eyes narrowing with suspicion. She was still regaining her composure from their desperate dash aboard the train.

"Just a hunch, I guess."

"Do you always act off your hunches?" she asked as he slid the door shut and sat down across from her.

"Not always."

"Well, how do you decide when to and when not to?"

"I don't know. I haven't really thought about it. Sometimes you just have to make a choice though. You don't always have every option available, and even if you did, you can't always know which is the best until looking back on the situation."

"Yeah, but I just wish there was more to it," said Sylvia, and she continued matter-of-factly, "I don't like going around making guesses all the time. Mother always said to think before I act."

"Well I think that's a good thing to practice," said Jacob. "Sometimes you just have to think quicker than others."

"I like taking my time," said Sylvia. "It's easier."

She huffed a sigh that covered the window in fog. Wiping it away, she could see the wall of water getting further and further away.

It was interesting that Jacob and Sylvia had been talking about thinking on their feet, because an opportunity to do so was just about to walk through the cabin door.

"What's going on here?" asked a tall, white-haired man as he burst into the room. He had a twisty mustache and wore spectacles, and Jacob's first thought was that the new arrival appeared to be dressed like a mailman.

"Nothing," said Jacob. "Why do you ask?"

"Someone pulled the Emergency Stop," he said with assurance. "The passengers in the lounge are complaining that you two had something to do with it. Now it is one thing to pull the Emergency Stop without permission, but pulling the Emergency Go as well, that is unheard of and explicitly disrespectful."

Now Jacob did not know what the word 'explicitly' meant, but he did understand that the tall mailman meant business; he had addressed the children with an air of absolute authority. The train was his realm and he was the undisputed ruler.

"We didn't mean anything by it, sir, honest," said Jacob, scrunching his face into as sorry and respectful of an expression as possible.

"Well, I suppose no real harm was done," said the man, suddenly softening, "But since I'm here, I should might as well collect your tickets."

Jacob and Sylvia looked at each other, hoping that the other would come up with some sort of clever pretext as to why neither of them possessed said tickets. No such idea surfaced.

"We don't have any tickets," said Sylvia frankly, also addressing the conductor with esteem.

"No tickets!" shouted the man, his face becoming grave once again. "Well, that won't do! You come aboard the Valiant Express, one of the most renowned locomotives in the world, and you pull the Emergency Stop and the Emergency Go, and you forget to purchase tickets! What sort of world are we heading towards if our young people cannot behave at least with somewhat decent sensibilities?"

"We are very sorry?" said Sylvia, scared that the man would raise his voice one more time.

"Where are your parents?" asked the man suspiciously.

Jacob's first reaction would have been to admit that their parents were not on the train, but considering the wall of water which chased behind them, he decided it would be best if they could stay on board as long as possible.

"I'm not sure," said Jacob. "They must be around here somewhere."

Sylvia gave him a look of frustrated questioning. He just nodded back in acknowledgement, raising his eyebrows as if to ask 'What else was I supposed to say?'

"Well, let me help you find them," said the man, opening the door and motioning for both of them to exit the cabin.

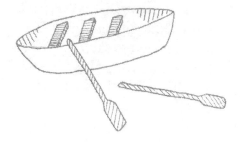

Chapter 8: Moab The Mouse And The Five Angels

The man rapped on the door two cabins over, which happened to be the best place he could have searched for the children's parents, considering it was the only cabin in which someone who had lost their children sat, frantic with worry.

"Do these belong to you, madam?" asked the conductor.

"Oh my babies!" shrieked the woman. "You found them for me! Thank heavens. I was positively beside myself. It's a fascination that I'm not sick from all the grief you two have caused me. Come sit down."

Jacob went in and sat down at the woman's imposing gestures and hysterical tone. Sylvia was confused but followed anyway. They sat across the cabin from her, wondering when she would realize her evident mistake.

"They say that they have no tickets," explained the conductor.

"Of course they don't! I have them right here," said the woman, handing three tickets to the man. "Now, find us some tea!"

"Right away madam," said the conductor, taking his leave and sliding the door shut.

"Now, Geoffery," began the woman, looking between the two children. "I said you could not go exploring until you finished your pictures. Start drawing or else I might start falling apart from embarrassment at my own child's lack of artistic accomplishments."

A pencil and notepad sat on the coffee table between them, so Jacob picked it up and began to scribble something on the pages.

"And you, Marcy!" the woman continued. "If you don't finish your reading, then how can you begin your next stack of books tomorrow? Now I believe you were in the middle of *The Disastrous Chronicles of Moab the Mouse*. Pick up that book at once, or else I shall keel over out of fear that you will never make something of yourself."

Shuffling a few items around, Sylvia found *The Disastrous Chronicles of Moab the Mouse* mixed within the pile of books spread across the cabin table, and she opened it to the marker stationed at page eight hundred and sixty-seven. Jacob leaned over to Sylvia, all the while keeping his eye on the woman.

"She can't see," he whispered.

"Can't see?" gasped the woman. "What can't I see? Tell me at once! Did you two spill that icky black coffee on yourselves again? I will not be responsible for my temper if I have to replace your wee outfits so soon after that last episode of caffeine chaos. Now tell me straight away. What happened?"

"Nothing," coughed Jacob, trying to disguise his voice with a raspy overtone.

"Good," said the woman, returning to her cross-stitching.

For a while, silence filled the cabin, except for the

occasional sound of what seemed to be the bossy woman's cross-stitch needle knocking against her nails. Tea was brought and the woman almost immediately ran the server out because of the length of time he took in preparation.

"Read out loud for a while, Marcy" said the woman, stirring a lump of sugar into her tea.

Sylvia uncertainly raised her eyebrows at Jacob, but he just shook his shoulders and pointed at the book. As she started with the first word at the top of the page, she tried to sound as ordinary as possible. Most children sound somewhat similar, but there are always those children to whom extraordinary voices have been given. Sylvia was accustomed to people telling her about her extraordinarily royal-sounding voice, and so she attempted to sound as common as she could manage.

"Chapter Twenty-Seven: The Broken Mousetrap," Sylvia began.

Moab the mouse struggled and struggled to free himself from his obsession for stealing cheese, but he could never overcome those tasteful urges that would spring upon him every evening around eight forty-five.

"What a dreadful rumbling in my tummy," said Moab. "I shan't find any peace tonight if I have not had my portion of that aged Muenster."

"Stop child!" shrieked the woman sitting across from Sylvia. "What on earth happened to your voice? You sound so much more pleasant and delightful than you did this morning. How dreadful! You ought to lay off the sugar in your tea today. Perhaps too much sugar is not good for your vulnerable vocal cords. Continue."

Sylvia continued where she had left off, trying even harder to sound less pleasant and delightful.

Moab, though wary of the dangers associated with saving his beloved cheese from the clutches of a horrid mousetrap, still determined to do just that. It was not simply the taste of the cheese that drew him to danger, but rather that there existed something extremely tempting about the idea of almost being caught. If the trap snapped and cut off some of his fur – all the better! It was almost as if he had a better sense of smell for the thrill than the cheese.

"I only wish ol' Spat was still alive to watch this," said Moab. "Even he would have been frightened at the state of this old trap. Its hinges look like they are about to burst on their own evil whim."

Moab thought back to the few months that he had known Spat. It was weird. Out of everyone who Whiskers could have eaten, Moab never suspected that Spat would be the one to get caught. He seemed like such a sly little mouse. Moab considered himself clever, but not nearly as clever as Spat.

"Oh well, I shall tell the others about it when I return to the nest," said Moab. "I don't need anyone watching me to enjoy this."

Sylvia paused, but the woman was so caught up in the click-click-clicking of her cross-stitching that she failed to notice. Jacob watched as Sylvia turned to the last page of the book and began to read it to herself. After a few moments, she bothered the woman with a groan of heated exclamation.

"He dies!" said Sylvia, clearly upset about what she had

just read. Her big brown eyes were squinted so hard that it was difficult for Jacob to see them. Her face was formed into a gloomy glower.

"What is the matter now? What are you talking about, child?" asked the woman.

"Moab dies in the end," said Sylvia, casting the book back onto the coffee table in the middle of the cabin.

"Of course he dies," said the woman. "That is the point of the story. But how could you know that if you haven't even finished reading it?"

"I read the last page," Sylvia answered.

"Well, you still have to finish the book nonetheless."

"Why would I want to finish a book that goes on for so long only to reach the end and find out that Moab gets carried away and eaten by a hawk? Children's stories should not end like that."

"Why not?" asked the woman, setting her needle and yarn on her lap, "Life ends like that, so why should children's stories end any differently?"

"Because life doesn't *have* to end that way," said Sylvia, barely disguising her distinctly superior accent. "And besides, stories like this just give you a bad feeling in your stomach and a sour taste in the back of your mouth."

"Everyone dies," said the woman. "It's the truth, child."

Jacob had yet to add anything to the conversation, and so without thinking, he threw an idea out that would help Sylvia's point.

"But not everyone gets picked up by a hawk," he said, carelessly.

What Jacob had forgotten was that he was not really the woman's child, and so he naturally would have had a different voice. Though the woman could not see, she could hear very well and she knew her children's voices distinctively. Sylvia had simply gotten lucky enough to be able to pass as the little girl whom she was pretending to be.

"Who said that?" the woman asked, suddenly disturbed at the thought of a stranger in the room. "Marcy, who else is in here? That is not Geoffery!"

"No, it isn't," said Sylvia. "That is Darnish, and I'm not Marcy. My name is Sylvia. We were pushed in here because we didn't have any tickets and we needed a place to hide out."

The woman was furious. She began to shake like a rather old power generator. The sounds she made were not unlike one either; she continued to sputter angrily upon the sudden entrance of the conductor, and he agreed to leave the rascals at the next stop.

"Well, at least we escaped the flood," said Jacob as the train pulled away.

"But we made that blind woman awfully upset," said Sylvia, glancing around at the landscape.

Everything looked almost the same as before; the major difference being that the wall of water was now too far behind them to see.

"That train must have been going really fast," Jacob remarked as they began walking down the road once more.

"I can't believe he dies in the end," said Sylvia suddenly, throwing out her arms in a heat of frustration. "That just doesn't seem right. I would never write a story like that."

"Some people like stories like that," said Jacob. "I think it makes them feel like their own stories haven't turned out so bad after all. Maybe it makes them realize what they really have to lose."

Interesting enough, Jacob was still unaware of what he had to lose. Now I know that most people would not want to be informed of the imminent death which awaited both Jacob and Sylvia, but I thought that it would be best if you knew. You might be thinking, "What? They cannot die. This story cannot end the same way that stupid Moab the Mouse story ended. Please don't say that was just a method of cruel foreshadowing." Well, if you were thinking this then I am pleased to say that they are not going to die like poor Moab. Though, it is possible that Moab could be loosely viewed as a metaphorical harbinger of certain events. You see, Moab the Mouse is eaten by a hawk. Jacob and Sylvia are going to drown, which is a completely different way of dying. If you are thinking, "That is even worse than getting eaten by a hawk," then all I can say is that I am sorry. I cannot please everyone, and it would be exhausting to attempt such a thing!

The two friends walked on for a few minutes until they came to a small bluff looking out over the waters of a petite little lake. A wooden sign read the name 'Theodore.' Moving along the shoreline, they came to a monument consisting of five small, bronze statues and an inscription reading, 'Where the Five Angels take their tea is where my heart shall ever be.'

"What do you suppose that means?" Sylvia asked.

Jacob read the quote several times and stared at the five little statues. They appeared to be well-dressed young aristocratic gentlemen. Each of them held a unique stature and pose, and it seemed almost as if they were frozen in the middle of a spurt of crippling laughter.

"I think the Five Angels are lakes," said Sylvia. "These statues are illustrations of their personalities. See. Under each of the statues is a name. This lake is named Theodore. He's the tall guy in the middle of the group."

"You are right," said Jacob, surveying the watery landscape ahead of them. He thought that he could make out another lake or two in the distance.

"So that's it?" asked Sylvia. "I thought we were going to find some answers. All there is here is a bunch of water."

"I don't think so," said Jacob. "Simplé said that we should ask our questions here. There must be more than this."

He walked down to where the water lapped up against the rocky shore. Discovering a boat, he climbed in and suggested that they take a trip over to the other side of the lake.

"What good will that do?" asked Sylvia. "I still don't think Mr. Simple had any idea what he was talking about."

"It's the only thing we have to go on," Jacob argued. "There has to be a way to escape that unspeakable creature of darkness, and I am not about to give up at finding it."

He paddled them out several hundred yards until

they were nearing the center of the lake. The waters battered against the sides of the boat as the wind picked up.

Now Jacob and Sylvia had completely forgotten about the wall of water, considering how long they had been on the train. Both of them had supposed it to have died out and no longer be of any threat, but I don't have to tell you how life's problems sometimes seem to resurface at the least opportune moments. This just happened to be one of those times, and as they paddled further and further across the lake, the flood crept up behind them once more.

If Jacob and Sylvia had realized that they were about to drown, I think their few remaining moments on earth would have been much less enjoyable. You might be thinking, "Well, if they had realized the flood was coming up behind them, perhaps they could have done something about it." But I assure you that there was no hope for flight in this circumstance. So the two friends paddled on in peace, unaware of the impending doom which ascended over the hills only a few miles away.

"I love that I can see my reflection in the water," said Sylvia, leaning over the side of the boat. "Mirrors are just not as accurate."

"Are you serious?" Jacob asked, befuddled at the strange ideas that often occupied Sylvia's mind. "Mirrors are far more accurate than water."

"I don't think so," said Sylvia. "Mirrors show us a clear and steady form, yet they miss the true nature of the human. The rippling darkness of the water displays a closer depiction of whom we really are inside. Our figure is corrupted by so many little quirks and calluses."

Jacob pondered Sylvia's statement. It was just plain confusing at first, but it slowly began to make more and more sense as he thought about it.

"I think you are smarter than me," acknowledged Jacob as he continued to row with a steady pace. "I would never have thought of something so philosophical."

"But you think of other things," Sylvia said, smiling

with encouragement, "Besides, I can't say that I would have ever thought of that if you had not been here. I probably would have just gotten bored with myself and missed noticing the reflection altogether."

"You are a good friend, Sylvia," said Jacob, his eyes glowing with admiration at his companion.

"So are you, Darnish," Sylvia replied, repaying the gentle look.

"Sylvia?"

"Yes."

"My name is not Dar..."

Suddenly, the wall of water hit the shore and produced a rippling wave, which spread across the entire lake. Jacob and Sylvia looked back in terror, but there was not enough time to manage any sort of escape. Jacob paddled as fast as he could, but it was not enough. The water lifted the boat up into the air and then brought it back down upon the surface of the lake with a crushing force. Jacob and Sylvia were enveloped.

Now I know that I informed you that at sometime the two children were going to drown. Well, this was it. I have to imagine that drowning is not a pleasant experience, but I cannot give you an accurate description of the process since I do not have any clue where to start. You will just have to imagine it for yourself, and if you get the chance, perhaps someday you could ask either Jacob or Sylvia what it was like.

Jacob felt himself swirling down into the depths of the lake, which now seemed to be an ocean of nothingness. His body was left somewhere behind as he moved through a mass which resembled water and then through a substance that felt like air. His sight had been taken from him, so all he had left were his feelings, and even they were numbed.

Chapter 9: Tea Time

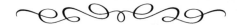

"Look at his little face," said a voice in Jacob's ear. "I don't suppose he is a very old human if his head is so small."

Jacob opened his eyes. He lay on what looked to be a whiff of cloud, feeling as if he were immersed in a heap of downy feathers. In front of him were two long sandaled feet at the bottom of two long legs leading to a long figure. At the top, which was very far away from where Jacob lay, was a familiar-looking face peering down at him. The gentleman had an awkwardly longish nose but a kind smile that made up for it.

"Join us for a spot of tea?" he asked.

"Okay," said Jacob, lifting himself to his feet and realizing that he was less than half the height of the lanky man.

"This tea certainly is something else," said Sylvia, who was perched up in the middle of an oversized sofa, which made her appear to be a miniature version of herself.

"Pour another cup," said the man. "This young gent

looks thirsty."

"I cannot imagine after drinking so much that he should still be thirsty," said another tall man, though this man was not as tall as the first.

"What do you mean?" Jacob asked.

"Well, why don't you have a seat and I'll explain," said the man, leading Jacob over to a comfortabe and well-used day chair.

As Jacob walked, the floor seemed to swirl and spread away from his feet. With an effort, Jacob lifted himself up onto the cushioned seat, feeling much the way a baby feels when it first begins to climb. Then the man began his explanation.

"You were drowned in Lake Theodore," he said, his manner being blunt yet tender.

Jacob choked on his tea, and quickly grabbed a napkin to cover his reddening face.

"And seeing as how I *am* Theodore, I feel somewhat responsible."

Jacob looked over at Sylvia, who appeared to already have a grasp on the situation. She bounced up and down in her seat, spilling a drop of tea over the rim of her cup. She watched with amusement as the drop lifted up and away.

"Why would you be responsible?" Jacob asked, trying to understand where he was.

"Because I am Theodore," said the man. "These are my friends, and we are the five angels that dwell above the five lakes."

"Four," one of the others corrected him.

"That's right, we lost one," said Theodore. "But this is Everest, Remington, and Clouse. And we were all just about to take afternoon tea when you two showed up at our doorstep."

Jacob looked around. Each angel was dressed in a top hat and a three-piece tuxedo. They reminded him of someone, but he could not think of whom. Everest was tall, but not as tall as Theodore, and he had a black curled mustache that matched his black wavy hair. The chubby angel was named Remington and he liked to sit and chuckle after every other sentence that was spoken. The fourth angel, Clouse, was younger and had a better physique than the rest. He had a wide chin and his face looked handsome and intelligent, but he hardly ever said anything at all. All of them, however, were about one and a third the size of a normal human being.

As Jacob continued to survey the room, he noticed that the floor and walls seemed to fade off as if they were nothing more than a fluff of cloud, and sometimes they blew away and were replaced by a different bit of haze. There was a large brass door set in a golden archway that lead off into an abyss, and in the center of the room sat a round Victorian-styled table, around which five similar chairs had once been evenly spaced. Now, the sofa, on which Sylvia sat, had been a recent addition to the uncharacteristically material furnishings.

"When we saw you topple under, we decided it would be best if you stopped by for a sip of English brew before you dashed off to the afterlife," said Theodore. "I thought I should attempt to make up for the ill fortune you happened upon in my lake."

"Isn't it lovely?" Sylvia asked Jacob, bouncing up and down in her seat once more and then again and taking another gulp of tea.

Jacob sighed a dull sigh and leaned back in disillusionment. "It's great," he said, "But we're dead."

"Yes but the tea tastes lovely, and the company is comparably refreshing," Sylvia sweetly contended.

"Have another scoop of sugar?" asked Remington, chucking bashfully at Sylvia's comment. "It really only gets better the sugarier it is."

"I think I will," said Sylvia, nodding politely. "We should stay here forever, Darnish."

"Who's Darnish?" asked Everest in amusement at the child's funny remarks.

"Well, he is," said Sylvia, pointing at Jacob.

"We don't want to stay here forever," said Jacob as he locked eyes with Everest, who produced a knowing stare at the flustered boy. "We want to go back," Jacob added.

Everyone in the room halted their present actions. Remington began to chuckle but then stopped shortly after realizing the serious nature of the silence.

"Go back?" stuttered Theodore. "Why on earth would you want to do that?"

"You mean, why in heavens would you want to do that," Clouse corrected him.

"Ah, yes. Thank you Clouse. Why in heavens would you want to go back?"

"Because I was charged with keeping Sylvia safe," Jacob explained, slumping at the realization of what he had done or failed to do.

"You don't get much safer than dead," said Everest kindly.

Remington began to chuckle once more.

"That is true," said Theodore. "Look at it this way. You don't have to worry about that anymore. Nothing untoward is going to happen to her now."

"I can't just leave it at that," said Jacob in defiance. "I made a promise to her father. I was meant to keep her alive and well. We didn't come here to die. We came here to ask you a question."

"A question? I like questions," piped Remington, who then proceeded to laugh at his own comment, which really wasn't funny at all.

Theodore rolled his eyes and inquired of Jacob. "What question, child?"

"We were told by Simplé the Wise that you would know how to stop the creature which pursues us."

"Simplé is not really all that wise, if I remember correctly," said Theodore.

Jacob ignored the comment as if he had not even heard it. "Simplé said it was called Destiny, and I was hoping that you would be able to tell me how to be rid of it."

"Well, you are rid of it now. He isn't going to pursue you here," interrupted Everest.

"But we aren't going to stay here," said Jacob. "I must find a way back."

"There is no way back," said Theodore, sternly. "Besides, even if there was I can't help you with your problem. There is no avoiding Destiny. If he is on your tail, eventually he will find you and eventually he will have his way."

"Couldn't you do something about it, though?" asked Jacob, almost beginning to despair. He looked around at each angel, hoping to find one who would pity him and his friend.

"Of course not!" said Theadore.

"We are just angels, after all," added Everest.

"Well then it's a good thing we've found our way up here," said Sylvia. "I should hate it if that creature ever really did catch up to us. He was horrid, I tell you. Simply horrid."

"Well, there is one way," said Clouse, suddenly speaking up. He had been consistently silent until that point, and it was obvious by the odd looks being passed between angels that his speaking was a rare occurrence.

"What do you mean?" asked Theodore, intrigued.

"I could go ask *you know Who,*" said Clouse.

"Well, if you really think it might do some good," said Theodore approvingly. "I do hate to see these poor children out of spirits."

"You mean in spirits," said Clouse, quickly rushing out of the room and into the open abyss.

"Ah yes, in spirits, exactly," Theodore admitted.

"Was he cold?" asked Remington, turning to the girl.

"Like ice," answered Sylvia.

Remington shivered and then chuckled his way back into a happy grin.

"What do you mean when you say you lost one?" asked Sylvia.

"What's that, child?" Everest asked.

"You said you lost one of your angel friends, and now there are only four of you. What do you mean you lost one?"

"Well, there used to be another. His name was Dawson, but he never fit in very well with the rest of us."

"You mean Dawson Quinn?" Sylvia asked excitedly sitting up in her chair. "We met him not too long ago."

"You did?" asked Everest. "Then you must have seen how uncouth and ill mannered the fellow was."

"Not at all," said Sylvia. "He saved me from being digested by a werebear."

"Well, he doesn't ever show up to tea on time," said Everest in slight disgust.

"And he's always forgetting to button the top button on his suit coat," added Remington.

"Terrible, terrible manners," said Everest disapprovingly.

After a few minutes, Clouse ran back into the room and began to whisper something into Theodore's ear.

Jacob had been sitting and contemplating the previous conversation for several minutes. He had a strange look of consternation on his face. "That doesn't make sense," he said finally.

"What doesn't make sense?" asked Theodore, leaning away from Clouse.

"What you said earlier doesn't make any sense. If Destiny eventually finds you, then why did he never find us?"

"He must have," said Theodore. "You ended up here didn't you?"

"But he was never there when the water hit us. Why wasn't he there when we drowned?" asked Jacob.

"Well," answered Theodore, his voice trailing off into a faint echo. "Apparently, that wasn't your destiny after all."

Clouse gave them a wink and then suddenly Jacob and Sylvia felt themselves being dragged backward out of their chairs and through a mist of cloud.

It felt like a lifetime to Jacob before he was once again able to perceive consciousness. The weight of an unnatural slumber hovered heavily over his eyelids as he drifted up and down the rocky shore. The slow awakening into a less than desirable reality brought a grave thought to his mind. He had no idea where he was meant to go next. He struggled to lift himself out of the icy water. The day had darkened and mist poured in over the lake. Jacob searched for Sylvia, running up and down the shore, unable to find the girl he had promised to protect. Finally, amid the strokes of lapping water brushing against the clefts, he saw her. Sylvia's face looked pale and cold as she floated up and down with the movement of the water. Drawing her out, Jacob carried her up the shore until they came to rest in the grass.

Now Jacob wished he could take Sylvia back to her father. He wondered if her father was still alive or if he had met his fate along with so many others. It seemed like there was no escaping the inevitable. If my memory serves me correctly, I think I told you earlier that Jacob's pursuer eventually gets the best of him. I'm reminding you now so that you don't get any fancy ideas about Jacob getting away. If there is one thing the five angels said that stuck with Jacob, it was that he could not escape Destiny, and Jacob was beginning to believe this. As he thought about their current situation, he wondered if there was any reason to keep going.

The two children had found themselves shivering in the cool of the evening air, lost as to where they should go. Jacob looked at Sylvia, who had still not opened her eyes or said anything. She just lay there, breathing slowly with her arms wrapped around herself, attempting to muster some sort of warm feeling. Jacob thought about what her father would have thought about him if he could see her now. He took off his shirt, which had begun to dry, and he wrapped her in it. Then he stood up, and with a newfound courage, he began to look around. Climbing a hill, he discovered a well-traveled road and in the distance he could see a light approaching amidst the gathering darkness. Running back down the hill, he aroused Sylvia from her sleep and helped the tired child climb the hill. Their hopes were raised with each upward step.

A wooden carriage appeared, bearing a single rider. Just as a plea for pity prepared to leap off Jacob's tongue, the carriage began to slow down on its own and came to a halt in front of the two children. The rider looked down toward where they stood on the side of the road. They were ragged.

"I suppose you will be wanting a ride," he said, with every other word drawn out into an exasperated sigh.

"Yes, we would most certainly," Jacob answered. Normally he would have watched his tone and level of directivity when speaking with an adult stranger, but Jacob was not taking any chances. They were cold, hungry, and tired. And they needed a ride.

"Well I can take you as far as the Miss' place, but no further. I'm afraid if she found out I trailed off to town before coming back she would have a fit, and I'm not in the mood for putting up with one of *those* right now."

"We understand," said Jacob, offering a boost to Sylvia, who sat herself beside the driver.

"I would let you ride inside, but she's filled to the brim at the moment. Just ran an errand in preparation for the Miss's niece's wedding, which couldn't come soon enough, if you know what I mean."

"Not really," said Jacob, with a sidelong glance at Sylvia.

Chapter 10: Miss French And The Boarding School

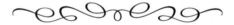

Now I would rather tell you about only the best parts of the story, and believe me, better parts are coming, but it would be wrong to leave the worst parts out because I am under the belief that they ultimately make the best parts even better. In holding true to this theory, I will continue with the scene we were presently in, but not before I warn you about the vile force of nature by which Jacob and Sylvia are about to find themselves assailed. Now I really couldn't care less what you might be assuming that I am referring to, and the less you think about it the better, so I will just break it to you as straightforwardly as possible.

"School," said Miss French. "Children should be in school. They need to be brought up with a solid education with the proper resources for developing normal aptitudes for understanding. The continuation of our pleasant social construct depends on it."

"Perhaps," replied Jenny, holding her tongue while similarly holding on to her less than traditional belief in the 'free thinking' movement of the decade.

Jenny was one for open opposition but only when it aligned with her chance at increasing her rank in society. Though Jenny had kept mostly quiet during her rant, Miss French knew from previous inquiries that Jenny maintained entirely opposite thoughts on the matter, and so when two apparently destitute, young, and assumingly impressionable children arrived at her door, she took it as the perfect opportunity to win an argument that had never even started.

"What have we here?" asked Miss French, glancing over the rim of her glasses at Jacob and Sylvia in their extremely unkempt state. Miss French spoke in a very high manner, enunciating each syllable slowly and with more than enough clarity.

"They were stranded on the side of the road, Miss," Henry the carriage driver answered. "They have no place to stay and I know you are not partial to random acts of charity, but..."

"Here is a prime example of what I have been talking about," said Miss French, pointing once at Jacob and once at Sylvia. "These two perceptibly uneducated young people have grown up in a world without school, and as you can see they are now paying the consequences for the inconsiderable choices of their guardians."

"I do go to school," said Jacob, innocently correcting the misunderstanding.

"So do I," said Sylvia. "Mother always made sure that I..."

"Tsk, tsk, tsk," interrupted Miss French. "See what I mean? This 'young lady' has no sense of manners whatsoever."

The two started to regret their decision to catch a ride with Henry, but a droning tiredness and worsening hunger overcame some of their frustration. Sylvia managed to speak up despite her emotional state.

"But we do go to school," she said. "The best way to be polite is to see the world from the other person's perspective and then treat them appropriately. If my manners seem less than adequate, it's just because I would not have wanted to be misinformed if I were in your position."

"Where did you find them?" asked Miss French, now thoroughly ignoring their soft voices and projecting even louder the piercing raspiness of her own.

"On the side of the road without a place to stay, Miss," answered Henry.

"There, you see? If you children had been in school, then you would not have been homeless, wandering around and adding to the blight of poverty already present in society today. The facts all point to you being unschooled, and everyone knows that the best remedy for something that isn't, is to make it so. So that my point will stand the test of time, I will make you two an offer. I will agree to send you to school if you will, in return, do your very best to improve yourselves with your studies," she stated with the air of a magnanimous benefactress, a disturbingly wide smile settling on her otherwise stern face.

Jenny nodded, impressed with Miss French's determination at convincing obsolete acquaintances of something so trivial.

Henry looked pleased.

"We don't want to go to school," said Sylvia. "We're just hungry and tired and cold and wet and that's all."

"Yes, its like I said before. We already attend school," said Jacob.

"Well, unfortunately, I have only given you one choice," began Miss French. "Either you attend school, where you will receive adequate food and shelter and a good solid education, or else I cannot bring myself to offer complimentary aid to strangers such as yourselves, no matter how poor and helpless your little selves may seem."

Jacob and Sylvia turned to each other to confer about the woman's offer.

"I just want something to eat," said Sylvia. "My stomach feels like it's going to implode, and I don't even think stomachs can do that."

"I know," said Jacob sympathetically, "At least they will feed us this way. I don't think we have any other choice."

"We'll do it," announced Jacob, feeling too tired and famished to argue any longer.

"It's a relief to know that children these days are not completely nonsensical," said Miss French. "Henry, take these children down to Sherwood Boarding School and tell the warden that I want them enrolled immediately. I care not how late it is. I want them prepared to start school bright and early in the morning."

"Yes, Miss," said Henry as he escorted Jacob and Sylvia out of the room.

"Can we have something to eat first?" Sylvia asked meekly as she was led out of the room.

"Nonsense!" she heard Miss French fume as they left. "School first. Eating second. Only students who have been properly taught should be properly fed."

This didn't make much sense to Sylvia, but Jacob reassured her that he would attempt to find something for her to eat before bed.

Henry drove them over to Sherwood Boarding School and persuaded an irritated warden to admit them into the barracks that night. Their supplies were gathered and they were each assigned to a bed in separate rooms. Jacob made his bed as quietly as possible for fear of waking the other boys in the small room. The other students were sleeping soundly. He then snuck out to the hall where he found Sylvia curled up in a wooden armchair.

"I'm hungry," she said weakly.

Just then, Henry pushed in the door at the end of the hall, his ears and eyes red and his coat covered in the dry patter of a freshly fallen snow.

"Sir," Jacob pleaded. "My friend is very hungry. You must understand that she has not eaten all day. I was hoping…"

Henry, already in the process of unwrapping a tea towel that he had been carrying in a small basket, suddenly produced several warm biscuits and a small tin of jam.

"It's all I could find at such a late hour," he said, handing them to the children.

"It's plenty," said Jacob gratefully.

The school was dank. Either that or the weather was so dank that the school also failed to be anything but dank. Jacob felt a sense of relief even though they were abruptly woken at an indecent hour by a crackly and alarming voice over the intercom, which announced that they were going to be fed a decent breakfast. Fortunately for them, the breakfast actually was decent – only lacking the warm smile of a mother.

Despite a display of cheerlessness around them, they were glad. Jacob and Sylvia received a helping of scrambled eggs and hot buttered grits, two slices of crispy bacon each, and a half piece of French toast drizzled with maple syrup and topped with clotted cream. Both of the children ate quickly without saying anything.

"I'm tired," said Sylvia as she finished her last drop of orange juice.

"At least you aren't hungry any more," said Jacob, slightly annoyed with her Highness' persistent complaints.

"No, but now I'm tired."

"Life isn't perfect," Jacob quickly responded as he began to place his head down on the wooden table but then stopped.

The furniture was nice. Sorry, let me try that again. The furniture was obviously the work of some expert craftsmen, and was so immaculately clean that Jacob didn't know whether to use it or not. The silky smooth edges of the waxed oaken table and chairs were carven with delicate flourishes and loops and the velvet cushions were a lovely emerald green. The two friends were beginning to realize that they had enrolled in a rather high-end establishment, and Jacob felt out of place. Sylvia felt right at home.

"Why not?" Sylvia asked out of frustration. "Why isn't life perfect? I mean, why can't it be? My life was perfect up until now." She thought about the days and weeks she spent running through the forest, unpretentiously playing and filling her time with seemingly endless and amusing adventures.

Then she remembered the nights when she and her father would build forts and ships atop his kingly bed and pretend to be explorers sailing across the vast blue linen sheets.

The words, "Your mother," almost slipped off of Jacob's tongue but he realized the severity of his potential comment just in time. The words were not needed, however, for the same thought had soon engulfed Sylvia's mind. Jacob watched her eyes for a few moments until he saw a sullenness encroach her thoughts.

"Life is terrible," said Sylvia, unashamedly flopping her head down into her hands and beginning to cry uncontrollably.

"Sometimes I think that too," said Jacob, "But..."

"But what?" Sylvia yelled. "You can't just say that and not have anything else to say!"

Jacob had always loved the word partition, and he had been trying such a long time to use it in sentence, and somehow he had at last found a way to use it. I don't have to tell you how he used it because you have probably already guessed that Sylvia did not share in his sudden amusement over his triumphant usage of arbitrary vocabulary.

"What on earth are you talking about?" she cried, tears still running down her face and dropping onto the embroidered silk tablecloth. She left immediately and spent the remainder of the scheduled breakfast time in the ladies' room. Jacob felt understandably guilty, especially when the first class of the day commenced and Sylvia was not present.

"We have a new student today, I see. My name is Mrs. Vicky Damperbottom, and I will be your primary daytime instructor," announced the imposing woman standing at the front of the classroom and looking right at Jacob. She stood tall, like a trained solder.

Jacob was enthralled with her method of projection.

"Now I want you all to take out a sheet of paper and write down the single most beautiful thing ever written. You have five minutes. Begin!"

Jacob began to think about the most beautiful thing he had ever learned in school. Just as he was at the point of decision, weighing between the periodical table and the difference between a circumference and a diameter, Sylvia opened the classroom door.

"I'm sorry for being late," she said.

"And who are you?" asked Mrs. Damperbottom, surprised at Sylvia's insolence.

"My name is Sylvia," said Sylvia, with a graceful curtsy and gentle smile.

"Well, you are late, Miss Sylvia. Take a seat."

She quickly sat down in the desk next to Jacob, who leaned over and whispered the assignment to her.

The five minutes passed and the students were called one by one to the front of the class to read aloud their answers.

The first student stood in front of the class and recited a single stanza from a poem by Jonathan P. Carthage. It went like this:

The winter of my love
is as the warmth of a beating heart
For you have stirred even the
coldest of thoughts to life

And though you attempted
to break me from the start
My love will beat firm still,
though my frail body decides to die

Mrs. Damperbottom quickly scribbled something down and motioned for the boy to return to his seat. Then it was Jacob's turn. To fully understand his answer, one would have to first understand the sarcastic nature of his response. This should not be incredibly difficult for you, considering how long you have known Jacob. His answer was as follows:

The most beautiful thing ever written cannot be written by me. For as soon as I put it on paper, it becomes merely a copy or reference to the most beautiful thing ever written. Therefore, it cannot exist in the frame of display hereby presented.

"I doubt you learned to be a sass from your lessons. You learned that on your own," said Mrs. Damperbottom.

"He was not sassing you," said Sylvia abruptly, defending her friend. "He was simply looking at the question from another perspective. I thought it was quite clever."

"Oh, and I bet you think speaking out of turn is quite clever too I suppose," remarked Mrs. Damperbottom. "Well, I don't think it's clever at all," she spat. "You two, report to the office."

"The office?" said Sylvia. "But we just got here!"

"Please," pleaded Jacob. "We will try harder. I

promise."

"Where did you children come from?" asked the disconcerted teacher.

"We ran away from home," answered Sylvia.

"You ran away from home? Your parents must be terrified."

"My father knows," said Sylvia, reassuringly. "He told us to go."

"And where are you going?"

"I..." Sylvia was stumped. Neither she nor Jacob really had much of an idea.

"We don't know yet," Jacob finally confessed. He studied the teacher's appearance. His experience thus far had taught him not to expect clemency from her.

"So you ran away from home, and you don't have any clue as to where you are going? It is just like children to not know where they are going. That's all we need: more wayward youth who apply no sense of direction to their future."

"We don't need to know where we are going," Sylvia argued.

It was unlike Sylvia to speak rudely to her elders. She had been raised to behave respectfully and in adherence to the rules of the classroom, but she viewed this situation differently. She did not like being forced to do something that she felt was unfair. After all, she was a princess in her realm.

"And why not?" asked Mrs. Damperbottom, daring the children to answer imprudently.

"Because, we know *why* we are going," said Sylvia.

Mrs. Damperbottom was silent, her face reddening. Then, a sense of hatred issued out of her inner most being. The last thing that Jacob and Sylvia remember hearing before they went rushing down the halls and out into the snowy courtyard that sat between the schoolhouse and the cafeteria was her harsh voice bellowing, "GO TO THE OFFICE, AT ONCE!"

Now, the weird thing about adventures is that they can change in an instant. Without warning, something very different can happen that was not previously expected. Life is not inclined to give warnings. As soon as you think you've filled your bucket to the top, you realize that you are actually sitting in the bucket. And before you know it, life goes about pouring you out into an ocean of chaos.

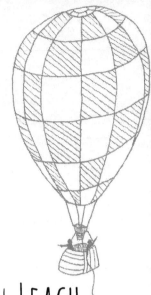

Chapter 11: Principal Leach and The Big Balloon

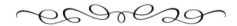

The children took their time in getting to the office, and upon brushing the snow from their shoes at the already powdered entryway, they announced their presence to a very small secretary behind a very big desk. After about a minute and a half of staring off into space, Jacob and Sylvia witnessed another boy from the class entering and handing the secretary a note. She in turn got up and delivered it to the room at the end of the hall. Then she sat back down and told them to take a seat.

"The principal will be with you in a minute," she said.

"I've never been to the office before," said Sylvia quietly in Jacob's ear.

"I have," said Jacob. "It's not fun. They yell at you and threaten to send you home and even spank you sometimes."

Jacob's thoughts were mingled with a much heavier subject, but Sylvia did not reason past his monotone remark.

Sylvia thought about what he had said. "I could handle a spanking if they would agree to send me home," she said. "I very much dislike being yelled at, however. I hope they just decide to leave that part out. If we're lucky, we may even get to see my father by early afternoon."

"I don't think so," said Jacob.

"Mr. Leach will see you now," the secretary whispered, motioning to the door at the end of the hall.

They pattered off, not very merrily, toward the principal's office. The lights were dim and it was very frightening and his name was Leach so that made things worse and I'm sure you can imagine it all for yourself. You seem like a bright enough individual to figure the rest out on your own, so I'll skip the simple details surrounding the scary aura that proceeded from behind the principal's desk.

Now that leaves us at the point of introduction. No, we'll skip that too. A little further ahead we find Jacob and Sylvia dumbfounded at the awkward behavior Mr. Leach seems to constantly portray. However, I've got something else to talk about at the moment, so I'll get back to that in a second.

Now seems like a good time to discuss the issue of story development. Story development is all good fun and it involves so many clever ins and outs, if you know what I mean. Stories go until they stop and then they are no more. As soon as they are done, you are left with nothing more than perhaps a simple point and the details are left to fade away as if they had never existed at all. That sums that up. No? I see. Let me have another go at it. I'm talking about the difference between false stories, true stories, and genuine stories. False stories are counterfeit and no one cares to mull over their worth long enough to recognize it. True stories can be vastly educational, and they often draw out a greater sense of authenticity. Genuine stories, on the other hand, may be true or false, but either way they cannot be changed. There is little development because all that can be developed has already been. They don't write themselves. They are already written.

And that is that. Well, if or not, I don't care. I say all this to say, the details are not important in this case.

Mr. Leach had a point to make. He slunk across the room and shut the door. He then sat down, leaned all the way across his desk, until he was no more than a foot away from the two children, and whispered something odd.

"I've got to get out of here," he said.

Suddenly, a curtain of angst was stripped from the children's imaginations. Jacob and Sylvia did not look over at one another, though the same thought did occur to both of them simultaneously.

"Have you ever had a dream?" asked Mr. Leach, rising to walk about the room until a hanging map on the wall detained his attention.

"Yes, I had a dream just the other night," said Jacob. "There were spiders and mountains that came to life and shooting stars threatening to..."

"No, I'm talking about a dream, like a fire," said Mr. Leach, turning toward them and waving his hands in such a way that the children began to assume a level of lunacy to his manner. "I'm talking about a passion, a goal, a hope that won't let itself die."

"You sound like my father," said Sylvia. "He's always talking about that sort of stuff. My mother used to say to him, 'Don't speak of ideas and then sleep in past them.' I never knew what she meant, but he seemed to understand."

"That's exactly what I'm talking about," piped Mr. Leach. "I'm sitting around here working my life away while I let a dwindling aspiration lull itself to sleep. I heard its song at a young age and now look how old I've become! Twenty-seven years since its first note has taught me one thing; A dream sedated unfurls a nightmare, and even worse yet – a delusion."

"You're not making a lot of sense," said Jacob, peering pensively at the door.

"I don't mean to make sense. I mean to make a change," said Mr. Leach, taking a quick look through the windows to the hall and realizing how elated his voice had become. He pulled tightly shut the blinds. "We must speak more softly. Tell me... you children want to leave, correct?"

"Well, sort of," said Sylvia.

"Why should we...exactly?" asked Jacob, being very careful in his wording for fear of upsetting the vibrant man. "I don't necessarily want to be here, but neither have you made a very good argument that we should think to listen to you."

"You are right," said Mr. Leach, calming himself and taking a seat behind the desk once more. "Let me tell you the whole story."

"I love stories," said Sylvia. "Well, that's not really true. I just love stories with happy endings and the ones where someone finds something they were missing for a very long time."

"Well, this isn't much of a story then," said Mr. Leach, attempting to cater to the young girl's musings. "But this is my point. When I was seventeen, I had this idea to create a product that would change the world. So I went to thinking up idea after idea. After months of thought and planning, eventually I landed on this."

If you are unable to reason how old Mr. Leach happened to be on your own, let me help you. He is at that age one reaches when they add twenty-seven to seventeen. If you are still unsure what age that may be, just know that it is in this case an age of reawakening.

Mr. Leach held up a rather strange looking object. I would describe it to you, but I assume that you are not a stranger to very well meaning people who have very bad ideas. I will say this much, so that you are not the least bit confused as to what Mr. Leach held out on display for the two curious children: It was a very bad idea.

"What is that thing?" Sylvia asked, attempting to cater to Mr. Leach's enthusiasm.

"Looks kind of cool," said Jacob. "What does it do?"

As soon as Mr. Leach had finished an impassioned rant about the function, fashion, and clever intricacies of his invention, he asked, "What do you think?" His face was bright with perspiration.

"It's stupid," said Jacob candidly. Jacob did not actually use the word 'stupid,' but his fairly polite attempt at finding a less offensive word ended up sounding a lot like the word 'stupid' to twenty-seven years of simmering ambitions.

"Well, I don't care what you think," Mr. Leach snapped. "It's going to change the world."

"I think it could," said Sylvia, attempting to bring a glint of encouragement to a man with a very bad idea.

"Well, it will," stated Mr. Leach once more. "But never mind what you say about it. What matters is what they say about it."

"They?" asked Jacob.

"Yes, they," said Mr. Leach, his eyes sparkling. "Everyone knows that they – the people that matter most – can be found in the tallest tower in the largest city. So that is where I'm headed. I'm going to sell my idea, and I want you to come with me."

"Why would you want us to come with you?" asked Jacob. "What on earth could we possibly have to do with any of this?"

Sometimes questions make a lot of sense to the person asking them, but fail to make any sense to the person being addressed. You may be thinking, "Jacob's question makes plenty of sense," but perhaps you haven't managed to think about it from another perspective. Mr. Leach had spent so much time developing his plan and going over it again and again in his mind that he had forgotten that Jacob and Sylvia really had no idea what he was talking about. It seems that relationships can generate a similar rift in understanding due to the fact that ordinary people have a very hard time reading each other's minds. One person may dwell on an idea or feeling for so long that once they end up expressing it, they forego explanation because they assumed their chum was already thinking the same thing. And then other times people seem to get into the habit of speaking much too loudly while flailing their arms and getting red in the face. I'm not predisposed to such activity, but it seems that a lot of people enjoy it a great deal.

As it happens to be, due to the fact that I seemed to have gotten somewhat sidetracked, Mr. Leach managed to finish explaining his plan to the two perplexed children. I will try to quickly fill you in. Mr. Leach planned on venturing to the tallest tower in the largest city, but he didn't really have any idea where either of those things might be. So one day when he came upon a broken down air station at the top of the hill behind the school, a brilliant plan sprung into his mind.

Upon investigation of the air station and after several minutes of inner turmoil, he resolved to fix what was left of the plane that lay inside and use it to fly really, really high up in the air. Once aloft above the clouds, spotting the tallest tower in the largest city would take but a moment's effort, and he would soon be on his way to sell his idea.

"That still doesn't explain why you would need us to come," Jacob interrupted, bringing Mr. Leach's rambling to a halt.

It seems that we have caught up to the rest of the story, so I will leave you in capable hands. Just don't expect Mr. Leach's ideas to lead him anywhere good. I'm not one for spoiling a good twist, but I just can't sit by and watch you think that perhaps Mr. Leach will ever escape what he considers an unceasing lack of success. Nor can I inspire you to hope that he will find any sort of life in the largest city that he propels himself toward. Instead, I must warn you of his fate. Let's just say, soon there will be a very bad end for a man with a very bad idea. Neither should you think that I enjoy such knowledge. I grow tired of telling you what you must know, for in order to caution you properly I must know it as well – and it makes me sad.

Mr. Leach returned a hasty description of his need. "Well," he began. "It quickly occurred to me that I had no idea how to fix a plane at all. So then when I discovered an old balloon as well, I was relieved at its simplicity in comparison.

With a little research and a lot of sewing and cross-stitching, I was able to bring it to a mend."

"How is a balloon going to help?" asked Sylvia, even more confused than before.

"He means a hot air balloon," said Jacob. "You can ride in those."

"Oh, that sounds romantic," she replied, with a deep sigh.

Mr. Leach and Jacob were both sort of struck by Sylvia's comment, considering neither could see the connection between romance and a large patched up balloon. Also, 'romantic' still happened to be one of those adult words Jacob didn't really understand and had trouble spelling on most occasions. It had been years since Mr. Leach had been romantic, and, as it was, he also had little care for the word.

"What I need you children for is to help me get the balloon up in the air. You see, I have discovered that it is a most difficult task to accomplish alone."

"So, if we help you take off, you will take us to the large city?" asked Jacob.

"Exactly," quipped Mr. Leach, riled with enthusiasm.

Jacob thought it seemed like a pretty good idea, and after getting Sylvia's input he agreed that they would help. Mr. Leach, in a rant of excitement, resolutely packed his suitcase, brushed his teeth, filed a few final papers in the cabinet on the far end of his office, and buzzed the secretary to inform her of his hasty departure. When she asked him where exactly he was off to, he tapped his fingers against what would soon be a memory of a writing desk and seemed to respond in the form of a question. "To the... super market?" he puzzled.

"How should I know?" the secretary replied. "*Are* you going to the super market?"

"Yes," said Mr. Leach, now confidently backing the ruse. "I'm going to the super market to pick up some eggs."

"Just remember you have a meeting at four," said his secretary, indifferent to his sudden urge for super market eggs.

"I will remember," said Mr. Leach, giving out a sort of

chuckle. "I couldn't possibly forget."

He laughed once more, and suddenly the line went silent. He turned to the children who were by now beginning to wonder what sort of man they had joined up with.

"Well, we're off," he said.

Good gracious. I just realized how terribly awful this must be for you. You have been stuck in a principal's office – though an office belonging to a slightly disturbed and abnormal principal – for quite some time now. It will thrill you to learn that a bit of excitement is just around the corner. Who it will not thrill so much is Jacob and Sylvia. They were just beginning to think that they had seen the last of their unwanted acquaintance named Destiny. I cannot start to wonder why they would be thinking such thoughts, however. It was previously stated to Jacob that one cannot escape their destiny, no matter how hard they try. Destiny eventually has his way, and I solemnly have to remind you that such will be the case for Jacob in the end.

"Darnish, are you sure this is a good idea?" Sylvia asked.

"I'm not really sure," said Jacob, letting out a sigh of heavy thoughts and winding expectations. "I hope so."

The children climbed in Mr. Leach's shadow to the top of the air station and helped unfold the balloon across the launch pad. They pulled the cords that held open the skirt, allowing Mr. Leach time to prime the burners. Watching the process, they were amazed as the huge roll of fabric began to appear more and more like a very big balloon. Once it was properly inflated, Mr. Leach tied it off a few more times and began loading his personal items. Everything seemed to go dreadfully smooth. I use the word dreadfully because sometimes things seem to go so smoothly that a dread of error hangs steadily in peoples' minds. Though they knew not why, this dread encircled the minds of the three soon-to-be travelers as they hurriedly prepared for departure.

Tossing the last of his things into the wicker basket, Mr. Leach paused. His eyes shifted one way and then the other, and Jacob and Sylvia knew that something was up.

Suddenly, a voice echoed through the air station below. The sound resembled that of a sports announcer across a pair of old stadium speakers. "Percy Leach, please step out of the air station with your hands where we can see them."

Mr. Leach tripped over a roll of cord as he scuttled to the edge of the roof. Peering over, the three companions were made aware of the large-scale police force, which surrounded the building and extended into the field beyond it.

"What on earth?" Jacob exclaimed, with a prickly look at Mr. Leach.

"Where did all those people come from?" asked Sylvia with astonishment.

"Is this illegal?" Jacob asked, pointing vigorously at the bouncing balloon.

Mr. Leach was rubbing his hand against his sweat-covered neck. "Not necessarily," he choked. "I mean, perhaps leaving at all might be considered somewhat illegal, but I didn't think they would be here so soon."

"You mean you aren't allowed to leave?" asked Sylvia. "What a terrible, horrible way to live."

Mr. Leach missed what Sylvia had said. He was too busy untying the final two ropes that held the balloon to the launch pad. He leapt into the basket and motioned with both his arms for the children to follow. They dashed over to where the balloon was currently taking off, but they were not about to simply climb aboard.

"We aren't going!" Jacob definitively shouted.

The wind was beginning to pick up, and the blustering sounds mixing with the blast of the burners overpowered Jacob's voice.

"What?" Mr. Leach shouted back as the balloon began to lift up into the air and across the stretch of roof.

"We aren't going," Jacob shouted once more, following the bounding balloon as it moved quickly to the end of the launch pad.

"You have to!" Mr. Leach yelled. "They will consider

you an accomplice if you stay! You might not have realized it, but I just committed a horrible crime!"

Police had begun filing onto the rooftop from the opposite end of the air station, and without warning they began to take aim and open fire upon the two children.

"Never mind, we're going," Jacob said, grabbing Sylvia and pushing her up into reach of Mr. Leach's stretched out arms.

"Got you," said Mr. Leach, pulling Sylvia up into the wicker basket.

Just then, the balloon drifted off the last segment of concrete and was quickly caught by another swift gust of wind. Jacob stopped at the edge of the rooftop and wrapped his arms around an antenna, which protruded up from the ground below. The balloon had flown off the roof and was lifting quickly up into the air.

"I can't reach!" Jacob yelled, taking a second to look back at the uniformed officers who were closing closely in behind him.

Sylvia pushed one of the cords of rope over the edge of the basket and it flipped up right in front of Jacob. He took one step back and then two steps forward, and with one mighty thrust he leapt off the roof and grasp the rope with both hands.

"He's got it!" Sylvia shouted, in exhaust. "Hurry, pull him up!"

Mr. Leach began to hastily haul in the rope from which Jacob hung on with a fiercely tight grip. They were quickly gaining in altitude, and for a moment the three travelers began to feel easier about their chances of escape. Then the principal suddenly wrenched back in angst.

"What's the matter?" Sylvia asked, tugging on Mr. Leach's sleeve. "Why did you stop?"

Mr. Leach had forgotten what he was doing the moment his eyes made contact with what was being uncovered on the road down below. Amidst the ant-like proceedings of officers and soldiers, a rather hefty piece of machinery was slowly turning its long metal cannon in their direction.

"They've got a tank," said Mr. Leach, staring hopelessly off into thin air. "I didn't plan for that."

"What's the matter?" Sylvia asked again.

"They'll shoot us down for sure!" shouted Mr. Leach over the burst of the first cannon.

An explosion ripped the sky thirty meters in one direction from the balloon.

"You've got to pull him up," Sylvia begged. "He might get shaken off. Oh, please!"

Mr. Leach wouldn't move. His dreams were washing quickly down the drain of despair and he just couldn't bring himself to finish the task at hand.

Suddenly, Sylvia was addressed by a familiar voice from the other side of the wicker basket. She quickly glanced behind her, and to her amazement she met eyes with Dawson Quinn.

"Dawson!" she exclaimed in relief. "Dawson, we need your help! Darnish is hanging at the end of the rope and they are trying to shoot us down."

"I know," said Dawson, giving her a sort of endearing yet regretful smile that should have clued her in to the fact that something else was on his mind.

Sylvia didn't have time to study Dawson's facial expressions, however, because she was still very worried about Jacob.

"I will do what I can," said Dawson. "Just promise me one thing."

"Yes?" Sylvia asked, now curious of his heavy manner.

"Promise me you will at least try to stay away from this sort of danger in the future."

"I will try," said Sylvia.

Dawson lifted his brow and gave a quirky grin. Then he leapt back out the rear side of the wicker basket and vanished into thin air. The bursts of cannon fire were growing steadily closer and closer to the balloon. The cannon was now following at a rather steady pace along their path. Trucks of soldiers lined in behind and spread out across the roadways.

"Who are you talking to?" asked Mr. Leach, suddenly coming to his senses. In his moment of hopelessness, he had not seen Dawson come or go.

"To Dawson Quinn," answered Sylvia. "He's going to save us."

"I don't think there's anyone who can save us, child," Mr. Leach replied.

Sylvia reached up and slapped Mr. Leach sternly across the face. Her countenance suddenly changed resolution as she realized what she had just done. She had from an early age been firmly instructed by her mother to never slap for any reason, but, in this one instance, a passionate determining had welled up inside that she could not resist.

"Now, pull him up," she said, pointing down to where Jacob still hung on for dear life.

Mr. Leach, without saying another word, leaned over the side and began yanking Jacob up into the basket. Just as Jacob reached the top and joined his fellow travelers, the cannon fired one last time. The previous burst had been so very close to the balloon that it had shook Sylvia and Mr. Leach almost clean out. This final shot, however, would bring the balloon crashing down in an instant. Jacob, Sylvia, and Mr. Leach watched as the rage of fire hurled itself in their direction. It was only a matter of seconds, but sometimes a matter of seconds is all life needs to change its course. I don't have to tell *you* that. You already know what I'm talking about. As the cannon fire neared the balloon, it seemed to Sylvia and Jacob as if time had haphazardly decided to continue its fidgety trek in slow motion. Then, in the path of the fire, they saw him. Dawson Quinn materialized only for a moment. He appeared forty feet out in front of the balloon and then was struck from behind by the cannon that had been headed straight for the two children. He disappeared into the explosion, leaving nothing but a trace of smoke rapidly fading.

Sylvia didn't say anything. Neither did Jacob. They

simply stared into the smoke, wondering what had happened to their friend. Mr. Leach had taken no notice of Dawson, and so he let out a cheer of relief.

"That's lucky then!" he shouted, leaning out the side of the balloon and waving his hand in a triumphant cheer. "They'll surely have us with the next one though. I suppose it's just a cruel gesture of hope life is throwing at us."

Just then, Jacob noticed a familiar figure along the path below. Amidst the soldiers and trucks and rushing officers, Destiny drifted. It passed its way between the commotion, stealing the confidence of the soldiers as he moved.

"Something's happening," said Jacob, pointing down toward where Destiny could be seen moving quickly across the landscape.

Then, with a rushing roar, Destiny leapt up through the trees and out into the clouds, growing into an airy mass of enormous size. Color left the sky, and the winds began to change. A tornado was forming right over the shuffling of soldiers. A sheer blackness filled the beast of wind and devastation. To Jacob, it looked as if the very fingers of Destiny were rapped around the funnel, stretching its icy grasp toward the balloon.

"We're doomed," said Mr. Leach, swallowing his words with a nervous swell.

The trucks and men below were suddenly lifted from the earth and tossed this way and that, finding their end at the rush of Nature's bitter pant.

"We'll be sucked down its gullet for sure," Mr. Leach said, looking back and forth from one of the children's faces to the other.

"No we won't," said Sylvia, austerely. "We must find a way out of this. There must be something we can do."

"Can you make this thing go any faster?" Jacob asked, looking up at the burners.

"Not unless that torrent decides to blow us away," winced Mr. Leach.

Just then, an idea suddenly occurred to Mr. Leach that he had yet to conspire. "Perhaps," he thought. "It just might work."

"What just might work?" Jacob beckoned, attempting to hurry the dazed Mr. Leach's thought processes along.

"If I can just reverse the transfer of energy, it might just create the desired effect," said Mr. Leach, reaching for a brown leather satchel. He pulled his invention from the bag and began flipping it this way and that. He rearranged compartments to reveal an assemblage of wires. His strange invention soon began to spark and fizzle.

"How is that going to stop a tornado?" asked Sylvia as she peered up at the approaching terror in the skies.

A swarm of dirt and trees were filling the mass of wind and rampage, and everything began to grow blacker and blacker with each second.

"We only have a few moments left," said Jacob. "You'd better hurry."

Mr. Leach slapped the last piece in place and stood up, facing the horrid gust. Quickly strapping the invention onto the bottom of the burner frame, he motioned for the children to stand to the sides of the basket. Then he hit the switch.

"What is it supposed to..." began Jacob, but he was promptly carried away from his words. The balloon, without any sort of commonplace uncertainty, rapidly began a certain change in speed, hurling itself through the increasingly chilly air at a momentous rate (as far as balloon travel goes). Before the children could really understand what was happening, they found themselves several hundred feet absent from the tornado and quickly gaining distance. Out from the back of the strange invention, which sat lodged below the furnace, a stream of endless fire and light seemed to form.

CHAPTER 12: FLOOR ONE HUNDRED AND SEVENTY-THREE

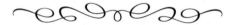

As they were propelled across the afternoon sky, Mr. Leach and the two children held on for dear life. The rush of air across their faces soon began to feel the norm, and their minds each drifted off to another place entirely. Mr. Leach envisioned his stunning success amongst the billionaire geniuses at the tallest tower in the largest city. Sylvia wondered what could have happened to Dawson Quinn. She thought perhaps he must have used some sort of trick or clever illusion to escape the explosion. Jacob thought about something else entirely. He remembered back to that moment in Sylvia's father's room. He thought about what he had said. Perhaps he would never have felt obligated to keep Sylvia safe without first hearing her father's earnest appeal, or perhaps it was only a matter of time. He now felt as if it was something else that stirred his heart. He just didn't know what. All he knew was that he at one time had a friend who he had done everything with, but then one day his friend had to move away. Now, he felt the same about Sylvia as he had once felt about his friend.

It is a strange thing, for a child to form a picture of true friendship or love or whatever you would call it without truly knowing what it is they have experienced. It seems as if children look so lightly upon friendship, only to later realize how heavy it must have been. And sometimes friendship never really matures to that point of helpless change until it's too late and both persons have moved on. Sometimes I think we miss people we never really knew. And other times I think we really knew people we never thought we had. Either way, Jacob knew something inside his way of being was beginning to change.

You may not realize it, but every part of Jacob's understanding is important to the story. Each second spent with Sylvia is eventually leading him to the makings of a decision. I don't really like giving away the ending before it's time, but in this case I feel as though I must say a few short things just to keep everything in order. You see, Jacob had originally embarked on this adventure for, well... adventure's sake. But if you asked him what the point of continuing was at the present moment, he may or may not have answered in the same way that he would have at first. He may have given a different response entirely – one that he would not fully understand until a little bit later. I say all this to say, Jacob would eventually be forced to choose. Neither should you forget about his unshakable fate. As I said, I don't really like giving away the end, but I must remind you that in the end he does indeed find his way into the death-dealing clutch of Destiny.

On a lighter note, the balloon was beginning to slow down. The air, at the same rate, began to feel more and more like it does when you've been standing out in the driveway far too long waiting for someone to come home on a winter's evening.

"We're in for some rough weather," said Mr. Leach, not

realizing the ironical nature of his own statement.

The children understood that the approaching mountain peaks meant snow and ice, but neither of them acknowledged Mr. Leach's comment due to the weighty thoughts that lay on their minds. Sylvia was the first to consider breaking the silence, but her emotions suddenly got the best of her and she broke out in tears. Jacob was alarmed.

"Sylvia, what is the matter?" he asked, moving over to her side of the balloon and taking a seat at the bottom of the basket next to her.

"I just can't help but think that Mr. Quinn is…" she began to say.

"I'm sure he's okay," said Jacob.

"Darnish, how can you say things like that? You don't have any idea and yet you just say it like it's true."

Jacob had forgotten that Sylvia still did not know his real name. He thought that perhaps it was time to tell her, but he feared what she might think. It really didn't matter any more. He knew that if he was going to continue being her friend, he would have to tell her the truth. As he began to utter the words, he felt as if his heart would burst through his chest.

"My name isn't Darnish," he said. "It's Jacob."

Sylvia's eyes narrowed as she looked him straight in the face. She backed her head away from his for a second, trying to get a clearer picture of his whole being. Then she said something that Jacob did not expect.

"That's weird," said Sylvia.

"That's weird?" asked Jacob.

"Very weird," she replied, giving him a little nod. Then she peered up out of the balloon at the darkening night sky, closed her eyes, and rested her head on Jacob's shoulder as if to fall asleep.

Jacob didn't think much about what she had said. He simply agreed with his own developing notion to always introduce himself as himself from then on. Jacob was glad to be who he was for the first time in this adventure. Even though someone had always known him as Jacob, now Sylvia knew him as himself as well. He felt at ease, and he couldn't help thinking that his being Jacob and not Darnish was somehow connected to what he was destined to do.

The night was long and chilly, and the three travelers bundled up to battle the harsh icy winds that sprung up over the slopes. Jacob and Sylvia eventually fell asleep, but Mr. Leach tested his perseverance against the cold darkness. Finally, a sliver of light etched itself across the horizon line.

"I can see it!" shouted Mr. Leach, forgetful of his sleeping companions' presence.

"See what?" Jacob asked, rubbing his eyes and lifting Sylvia's slumped head – replacing his shoulder with a sack of luggage.

Leaning over the side of the basket, Jacob could begin to see what looked to be the shape of a city skyline in the deep distance.

I would go into further detail about the journey into the city and about how they ended up landing on top of a diner (genuinely frightening several morning coffee goers), but really I just don't feel like it.

"Which floor?" asked the elevator attendant, stroking his strikingly straight and thin mustache.

"I'm not really sure," said Mr. Leach. "Just take me to the floor where I can sell this invention of mine. It's really quite amazing. See watch, if I..."

The lanky attendant, with a hint of boorish disinterest, stopped Mr. Leach mid sentence. "No inventions allowed to be demonstrated on the lift, sir," he lied.

"Oh, well..." began Mr. Leach, saddened. "I will put it away then I suppose."

"And you are looking for floor ninety-two, by the way" marked the attendant. "It's where all the inventions go after all the mulling, painstaking sorting, and eventual rejection has taken place.

"Yes, that's perfect," said Hanson Brown.

If you are slightly confused, let me attempt to disentangle the situation. After finding their way down from the coffee shop roof by way of a should-be-out-of-order fire escape, taking two buses seven blocks each and then walking another four, Jacob, Sylvia, and Mr. Leach had ended up directly across the street from where they had started, at the lobby elevator on the floor level of the tallest tower in the city. Another passenger, Mr. Hanson Brown was also taking the lift, and the three friends crowded the side of the lift opposite to him due to his incessant shuffling of the feet. The lift, although new as it appeared, portrayed the idealistic mark of emerging modern artistic influence mixed with the wealth of industrialization, taking Jacob unmistakably back to the roaring twenties where he had never been.

Mr. Leach peered over at the man standing in the elevator on the other side of Jacob and Sylvia.

"Please take me to floor ninety-two," Hanson Brown informed the attendant, fidgeting his feet left and right and dusting the shoulders of his suit.

Mr. Leach looked at Hanson Brown with a look of contempt. Mr. Brown was a stout fellow with charcoal hair and a pinched up face. "I suppose that's an invention of yours?" asked the former principal and recent renegade.

"You are absolutely correct," said Hanson Brown. "Though I would not tell you what it does for fear of scum like you thieving my life's work."

"Did you say ninety-two is where all the rejected inventions go?" Mr. Leach asked the attendant, trying to ignore the pitter-pattering steps of the nervous Mr. Brown.

"That's correct," said the attendant.

"That's the floor for me," said Hanson Brown. "Take me to ninety-two."

"No, we don't want to go to ninety-two," Mr. Leach corrected. "We want the floor where the inventions are submitted."

"Why?" Hanson Brown asked with an air of distain. "If they are only going to be rejected anyhow, it's better just to get it over and done with and take them straight to floor ninety-two."

"That's ridiculous," said Mr. Leach. "I thought you said that was your life's work."

"It is," said Mr. Brown. "And as soon as I can get it off my hands, I'll start a new life's work. Trust me. I've been doing this for years. Floor ninety-two is the one you want."

"He *has* been doing this for years," joined the attendant.

Mr. Leach was furious. "I don't want to go to floor ninety-two," he barked at the attendant. "Take me to the floor where I can sell my invention."

"In that case you want floor one-hundred and seventy-three," the attendant replied, punching in a few different big brass buttons.

"Strange people," Sylvia said. She leaned way over and spoke extremely soft so that only Jacob could possibly hear. Jacob only nodded in response.

Then it was time for coffee and cake.

Chapter 13: Coffee And Cake

Coffee and cake just happened to be the two most wonderful things in the world to a certain Henry Arnold Baxter Brimmings of floor one-hundred and seventy-three. Though impractical in every way, the first half of his average day was spent lounging around the office until 11:45 when the coffee and cake would be brought up from Bunting Bakery across the way down on street level. Mr. Brimmings had made so much money during his time that it no longer seemed to interest him, so day after day he did nothing until he had had his proper helping of cinnamon slice baked fresh to his taste and a decent cup of vanilla joe. This particular day was no different, and so it intrigued him to find two curious children in tatters standing at his door at 11:45 in place of the customary coffee and cake delivery lady.

"Bring it in! Bring it in!" he spouted, loosening his beautiful silk tie. "Fresh hot off the stove I hope?"

The two children stood in silence after making their way up to his brilliantly fashioned jumbo-sized desk. The desk was made of cherry wood and it was so glossy that the children could see their reflection on its surface. Jacob and Sylvia really had nothing to say, for they had not expected to find themselves standing in such a room addressing such a man. A few minutes earlier, the lift had brought them up to floor one-hundred and seventy-three. Mr. Leach, after issuing every sort of lie and clever reasoning he could imagine, had been directed into the big office where all the big investors sat around listening for (not *to*) big ideas. The children were allotted a bench in the hall, and after a few minutes they became frightfully bored, which in turn made them frightfully curious. In effect, that was how they ended up at the office door of a very elated investor whose coffee and cake were running late.

"We aren't supposed to be here," said Sylvia.

"Nonsense," snapped Mr. Brimmings cheerily. "You never know where you aren't supposed to be until you've been told to leave. And as long as you have brought that delectable cinnamon slice, I'm in no hurry to see you go."

Mr. Brimmings was a tall, handsome man of his mid-forties. His slicked back raven black hair matched the tone of his suit perfectly, and apart from the one red tissue in his jacket pocket, he was very dull in color. His charm and cadence made up for it. His posture was perfect, and the way he leaned forward made one feel as if he was always confiding a secret.

"Well, we haven't brought any," Jacob quickly informed Mr. Brimmings. "We don't even know what you are talking about. We were simply taking a quick look around and we noticed you have a very big office."

"Ah, you noticed I have a big office, eh?" piped Mr. Brimmings, intrigued at his peculiar guests. He smiled, leaning back in his chair and captivatingly placing his hands behind his head. "I've noticed the same thing myself on several occasions. It really is big, and it comes with everything an office should. I've got this huge desk that I don't know what to do with, complete with a Henry Arnold Baxter Brimmings cast-iron nameplate. There's a liquor cabinet over yonder, a French press on the butler's tray, and a lounge round the corner. And if you like the office, you should take a look at this view."

Mr. Brimmings strode over to the wall, which happened to actually be one really big window, and with a hefty yank he let fly the heavy damask curtains. Jacob and Sylvia ran over to the window. As they looked out, they both realized that they had never witnessed such a monsterously large city in their life. Buildings sat over there, and more buildings sat over here, and there were buildings packed behind and between those as well. The streets were bustling and the lights were flashing. People, people, and more people went this way and that, and there didn't seem to be one person who wasn't headed somewhere with a determined march.

"You like that view, eh?" asked Mr. Brimmings, triumphantly.

Jacob and Sylvia simply stared and stared, and Mr. Brimmings took their silent interest as a definitive approval.

"This is the tallest tower in the whole city," smiled Mr. Brimmings. "And I have the biggest office this side of the tower. Yes, children, I do indeed have a very big office," he kindly boasted, sitting back in his big chair and strapping his arms back behind his head once more.

"What does that mean?" asked Sylvia, pointing to a phrase marked above the inside frame of his office door.

"That?" asked Mr. Brimmings. "That's the motto of my life."

"It reads like an idiom," said Sylvia.

"What's an idiom?" asked Jacob, who figured his ignorance was simply a result of being sick one too many days the previous school year.

"An idiom is something that doesn't make a lot of sense," said Sylvia.

"Well, not entirely," said Mr. Brimmings, laughing wholeheartedly. "But you are very close. This however," he said walking over and pointing at the phrase marked above the door, "is not an idiom."

Mr. Brimmings cleared his throat and then began to read.

The greatest adventure is an endless one.

"Kind of short, isn't it," remarked Jacob.

"Not at all," said Mr. Brimmings. "Were you even listening? The greatest adventure is an endless one. Endless means never ending. It means it goes on and on and on and never finds a conclusion."

"That is so very sad," said Sylvia.

"Not if you are in the middle of it," said Mr. Brimmings. "Yes, I've stuck by that motto and look where's it has taken me."

"Is that why you keep the window closed?" asked Jacob.

"What makes you say that?" asked Mr. Brimmings.

"Well, it seems that if you are on such an endless adventure all the time, it must make you very sad to watch all the normal people down below who have never found such a life."

Mr. Brimmings stood up and peered down into a small park across the way. A young couple laughed as they watched their child slide down a small yellow slide and flip over off the end. They each put a hand around him, but he was quickly up and ready to do it again. At the other end of the park, a homeless man tossed a ball for his pup to chase. Passing by were two friends in the midst of a stirring conversation. They stopped to point the retriever in the direction of the ball.

"Yes, it makes me very sad," agreed Mr. Brimmings, strangely hesitant to take his eyes off the adventure that beckoned below.

I'm going to be frank with you yet again. Henry Arnold Baxter Brimmings had at one time lived by his motto. He had founded his business on the idea that life is full of adventure, but slowly over a long period of success, he had begun to feel as if there wasn't anything left. It was a growing fear of his – that his motto had failed to live up to it's potential or that somehow he had missed the adventure he had originally been destined for. But like most of us, Mr. Brimmings found a way to cure his desire for adventure by escaping his dreary existence through a piece of cinnamon slice and two cups of vanilla Joe every day at 11:45. On this particular day, however, something was different. The cake and coffee did not arrive at the usual time, and instead two curious children were now digging deep into the garden of his subconscious through the use of a few simple questions.

"What time is it?" asked Mr. Brimmings, flipping out a stunningly gorgeous gold wristwatch and following the tick-tocking hand with the rotation of his head.

It was 11:57, and the coffee and cake were nowhere in sight. Mr. Brimmings was furious, for not only was the coffee and cake late, but he was also in need of it to a greater degree than ever. There was really only one way to suppress the painfully raw ideas the children had just unearthed, and that was through a decent helping of coffee and cake. Mr. Brimmings began to call for his assistant. Instead of waiting for her to answer though, he suddenly marched across his big office, heading straight for the open door. Unaware that at the same time the Bunting Bakery delivery lady happened to be entering the open door from the opposite end, he made a sudden crash and a quirky fling into her arms. The coffee spilled, but just a bit. The cake she caught with her one free arm before it flew out of her reach. Then the two people struggled to pull free of each other and regain their ordinary posture.

"You're late," said Mr. Brimmings.

"I'm sorry, sir," said the woman, who now handed the

cake and coffee to the expectant investor. "It's on me today," she said, making a quick turn to leave.

Mr. Brimmings looked quizzically after her as she walked down the hall that led to the lift.

Then she turned right back around and pulled a handful of napkins from her flower-patched apron.

"Don't forget your napkins," she said, holding them out to Mr. Brimmings, who had now completely forgotten about the coffee and cake that had just been delivered. He stood there for a second and no more, looking down at the napkins. Then he looked up at her nametag and then at her. Her eyes were dazzling and everything else that makes a girl beautiful also dazzled too.

"Mary, do you like coffee and cake?" he asked, suddenly realizing the strange nature of his inquiry. "Well you probably have had enough coffee and cake for a lifetime," he muttered. "Do you like Italian? Would you like," he paused but only for a second and then continued, "to go out for Italian sometime?"

Mary smiled and then raised the napkins so that he would take them. He took them and then she left. Mr. Brimmings walked back into his office and set the packages on the big desk of his.

"Coffee and cake?" he asked the children.

"Yes, please," said Jacob, helping himself to a large piece of the delectably crumbly butter cake.

Mr. Brimmings went over to the window and peered down once more at the bustling world below.

"It's too bad she said no," said Sylvia. "She seemed like a really nice lady."

Mr. Brimmings was lost in thought. After a few moments, he looked at Sylvia with a smile.

"She didn't say anything," he said, a twinkle in his amber eye. "She has been delivering coffee and cake to my door every day for five years, and I have never once noticed her. But that means one thing."

"What does it mean?" asked Jacob, shoveling the last

piece of cake in his mouth.

"It means she will be back tomorrow, and perhaps tomorrow she will say yes."

"It certainly is possible," said Sylvia. "She did seem to have that…certain look in her eye."

"What look?" Jacob asked, imagining that this also had been a subject of conversation discussed on that day when he had been sick from school.

"You know," said Sylvia. "It's that look adults have when they feel something that they won't express.

"I hope you are right," said Mr. Brimmings.

Sylvia was right. She knew exactly what she was talking about. Mary did have that look in her eyes; but, unfortunately for Mr. Brimmings, he was about to lose his chance at finding out. For what neither he nor Mary nor either of the children knew was that a terrible fate awaited the busy metropolis, one that gathered itself for assault deep in the earth below. One individual who would have even less pre-warning was the tactful Mr. Leach, who, at the same time as Jacob was enjoying a bite of fresh cake, stood in the adjacent room defending a less-than-desirable object of discussion.

Chapter 14: Out To Sea

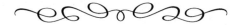

"But wait! There's more!" cried Mr. Leach under a gasp of pressure.

"That's quite enough," one of the fancy businessmen in fancy suits round the long meeting room table cut in. "We've heard enough. It has some potential, but it just doesn't seem marketable right now. You have no target audience and your current price range is ridiculous. Perhaps give it a few more years. Maybe go back and rework it."

Mr. Leach didn't answer. Going back and reworking it for a few more years may sound like a viable option to someone like you or me, but to Mr. Leach it meant failure. He had no home to go back to, and to see his invention rejected now meant he was through with it all. It meant no more inventing.

"Look, we can tell you are upset," joined in one of the other businessmen. "It's too bad Henry Brimmings isn't here. This seems just like the type of idea he might find interest in. Unfortunately, he doesn't see people until after he has had his late morning coffee and cake."

Just then, Mr. Brimmings, followed by two very excited children, burst into the room.

"Where is it?" he shouted.

"Well, here he is now," said the businessman.

"Where is what?" asked another one of the reluctant patrons.

"Where is that presizematograph, or whatever he called it?" Mr. Brimmings asked while digging through a cabinet of all sorts of odd-shaped devices and trinkets.

"You mean the presizemagram?" asked another investor, curious as to why Mr. Brimmings would be suddenly interested in such a thing.

"Yes, the presizemagigy, exactly!"

"It's in my office," said another investor, casually. "I wanted to test it out but I couldn't get the darn thing to light up. Perhaps the batteries were dead."

Mr. Brimmings dashed off. The two children followed once more, and so did the expectant Mr. Leach, who now realized who in fact it was that was causing the ruckus.

"What did you mean by 'It never affects this tower,'" asked Jacob, pursuing Mr. Brimmings hotly down the hall.

"I meant that the quakes are never big enough to give us a shake," he replied.

"Well, how often do they happen?" asked Jacob.

"Oh, every other day," said Mr. Brimmings. "You two children haven't been in the city long I take it."

"No sir," said Sylvia, helping Mr. Brimmings search the random office they had just barged into.

"Here it is," said Mr. Brimmings, holding up a small box-like device with a tiny screen and some cleverly placed knobs meant for switching, turning back and forth, and going beep-beepety-beep.

"What does it do?" asked Jacob.

"If I can have a moment of your time, Mr. Brimmings," interrupted the faint Mr. Leach, who now stood at the doorway. "You see, sir, I have this invention and I..."

"Batteries!" Mr. Brimmings interrupted. "Does that thing have batteries? Can I borrow them?"

Mr. Leach looked down at his invention. He hesitantly removed some batteries from one compartment and some more from another and handed them to Mr. Brimmings, who quickly shoved them into the preseismometer in his hand.

"You see," said Mr. Brimmings. "The earthquakes happen every other day, and everyone here is terribly used to it. But if you haven't been around, you would probably have no idea."

"Why is that?" asked Sylvia, curious as to where this conversation was headed.

"Because we rebuild every other day as well," replied Mr. Brimmings.

"You have to rebuild this tower every day?" she mumbled.

"That's my point. *We* never have to rebuild because this tower is so large and so well built that it never even feels the shake. It's only the smaller buildings and businesses and homes that feel the effects of the damage, and they are quite used to the reoccurrence. It sounds dastardly I know, but to everyone around here it really is quite normal."

Mr. Brimmings stopped and starred up at the corner of the ceiling for a few moments as if he had forgotten all about his present task and said, "Of course, the bakery across the street never feels the shake either. I donated a large sum of money to have a shock-absorbing frame put in. I didn't like that they were having to shut down every other day along with the rest of the city for repairs."

"I still don't see…" began Sylvia.

"It's working," shouted Jacob excitedly, pointing at the little screen on the preseismometer.

Mr. Brimmings twisted some of the knobs and switches and waited as the machine made several distinct sounds and then displayed what looked to be a graph of sorts. The two children and Mr. Leach watched as the expression on Mr. Brimmings' face altered. He drooped his head and walked about the hall until he came to his own office, and then he sat down in his big chair and looked out the big window. He let out a great big sigh as Jacob, Sylvia, and Mr. Leach entered the room. Through the side door came shuffling in all of the businessmen in their fancy suits.

"What is the meaning of all this?" one of them asked. As Mr. Brimmings spun around to face them all, he let out a sigh of dismay. "Perhaps I should explain," he said.

"Explain what?" Sylvia pouted. "We don't even know what you are talking about."

"Well, as most of you know," began Mr. Brimmings, "Our fair city is plagued by an unhealthy amount of earthquakes. I have never bothered to care in the past considering our building is so large and well built that it would never know the difference."

The roomfull of gentlemen gave a sudden acclamation of pride and some of them felt the urge to adjust their collars and de-ruffle their ruffles.

Ignoring their strange conventions, Mr. Brimmings continued. "And up until today, I never thought I would know the difference either. But at exactly 12:05, I felt the first shake that I have ever felt while standing in this building."

Murmuring dashed through the crowd of gentlemen.

"What on earth are you doing, Murmuring?" asked Mr. Brimmings. "We are discussing something important."

Mr. Brimmings' assistant stopped and steadied herself. "Sorry, sir," she said as she left.

"As I was saying," began Mr. Brimmings. He looked around at several frightened faces. "Never mind what I was saying," he said. "I suspect we are all going to die."

"Die?" Mr. Leach squeaked.

"Yes," replied Mr. Brimmings. "You see, this seismatomgrapher or whatnot is supposed to predict the size of the forthcoming quake. This line in the middle of the screen is supposed to show the largest earthquake ever recorded, and the line of prediction is blasting clear out the top of the chart."

The gentlemen stood round for a few moments gathering the knowledge and processing it to the point of understanding, and then panic ensued and they rushed off in several directions.

"We may still be safe in this tower though, correct?" Mr. Leach asked.

"Well, perhaps, but I doubt…" Mr. Brimmings stopped. Then he dashed off as well. "I've got to find Mary," he yelled.

"I can't die," whined Mr. Leach. "I haven't done any of the things I wanted to do with my life. I haven't even sold my invention yet."

As the children watched, he fell to his knees and stared plainly out the window. "I haven't ever been married. I haven't ever visited any of the places I wanted to visit. I've never made a name for myself, or built anything in honor of anything else, or come up with an idea that changed the world. I've never even come up with an idea that changed my life. I can't die. I just can't."

"Everyone dies someday," came an eerie voice that echoed in from the hallway.

Jacob peered out into the hall. There didn't seem to be anyone there. Suddenly, Mr. Leach's tone changed.

"I'm getting out of here," he said. "We've still got a chance."

Running from the office and down the hall to the elevator, Mr. Leach completely forgot his invention on Mr. Brimmings' big desk. I tell you this, not to foreshadow any sort of use for the item later on, but to instead inform you of Mr. Leach's troubled state of mind. You see, when people are brought to a state of panic, their priorities seem to find a way of ordering themselves without warning. In Mr. Leach's case, his lifelong invention paled in comparison to his survival. In Mr. Brimmings' case, though he had for five years never given her so much as a wink, he now made the decision to protect a certain lady that he knew very little about and whose affections were presently unknown. The businessmen in fancy suits now huddled inside their vaults and safes, reasoning that they had no desire to survive if their money did not survive along with them.

Mr. Leach rapidly pressed the lift button once and again. Sweat poured down his ruddy cheeks.

"Where are you going to go?" asked Jacob, who now stood behind him. "I just looked down into the streets. The roads are completely backed up, and there doesn't seem to be any way out. Everyone down there is in an uproar."

"I've got to get out," said Mr. Leach, unaware of whom exactly he was addressing. "I can't die," he repeated once more.

Then, the same eerie voice that they had previously heard repeated its response. "Everyone dies someday," it said, though this time its sound rang out in a more familiar tone.

"I know that voice," whispered Jacob, nervously.

Just then, the elevator stopped at their floor and the door creaked open. The lift was pitch black, but Jacob could see the swirling outline of the icy creature named Destiny hovering inside.

"The lights are out," cried Mr. Leach and he stepped past the lift doors.

"No, wait!" shouted Sylvia, but it was too late. Mr. Leach's body suddenly seemed to be yanked inward and disappear into the darkness.

At the same time, Jacob leapt toward the lift and slammed his fist against the close-door button on the inside wall. Then he grabbed Sylvia and sprinted back to Mr. Brimmings' office. As he closed the door, he glanced down the hall to witness what looked to be claws sliding down between the semi-ajar elevator doors.

"Lock it!" shouted Sylvia.

Jacob shut and locked Mr. Brimmings' office door, and then he did the same to the door across the room.

"Oh, it's coming back!" yelled Sylvia. "What are we going to do?"

This was another opportune moment for Jacob to admit that he didn't know what they were going to do, but after using the phrase so many times in the past and it never seeming to help anything, he decided to simply keep himself composed and think.

I must apologize for something I said previously. I may have alluded to the idea that Mr. Leach's invention would not come in handy again. If I did give such an impression, I am sorry. But in my defense, I could not have possibly known what exactly Jacob would come up with in such a rustled state.

Seeing as how he now was in such a state, Jacob drew from his memory how the invention had helped them before.

"Stand over there!" he brashly told Sylvia, pointing toward the window.

Jacob attempted to alter the invention the same way Mr. Leach had done while in the balloon. He wasn't completely sure if he was putting the right wires in the right places, but he didn't have time to contemplate the conversion. He added the batteries, and after a few adjustments, it sort of looked how Mr. Leach had made it to look.

Then the knock on the door came. It was a slow, creaky knock, and it filled the children with a sullen uneasiness. The handle fell clean off and the door opened. Destiny stood in the archway directly below the words, *The greatest adventure is an endless one.*

"You don't scare me!" Jacob shouted in defiance to the unwavering darkness. "I made a promise to protect Sylvia and that's what I'm going to do."

He lifted the handle on Mr. Leach's invention and prepared to pull it back when the voice of Destiny echoed forth.

"She is no concern of mine," it said, forcing its words out as if they were fallen leaves caught in a wisp of air.

"No concern?" Jacob asked, lowering the contraption.

"I'm here for you," said the voice. "Jacob, I've come to take you home."

"Take me home?" asked Jacob. "I don't understand."

"Everyone goes home someday," said Destiny.

"You mean everyone dies someday," said Sylvia, for

a moment allowing her gaze to cast itself across the evil creature.

"Yes, that is true," said Destiny. "Home is a strong word. Death – not so much."

"Who are you?" Jacob asked, squinting his eyes and peering as far into the darkness as he could manage.

"I am the angel of death," answered the creature, his voice trailing off as if it ceased to exist immediately after heard.

"It wants to kill you, Jacob!" Sylvia shouted.

"You can't escape destiny," said the creature, beginning to drift toward the two children.

"I know," Jacob whispered through his teeth, lifting the invention toward the consuming darkness.

He pulled the trigger. A burst of light and sound emitted from the end, and the room resonated with a pulse of antagonism. Rays of fire blocked the path of Destiny, and the creature crept back into the hall. As streams of light surged all around it, the dark angel succumbed to the powerful blasts.

"It's working!" Sylvia shouted as she stepped toward Jacob.

"Stay where you are!" Jacob yelled as he motioned for her to back up.

He was able to push the wall of blackness back down the hall, and for a second he thought they might have a chance to escape. But unfortunately for Jacob, there was no escaping Destiny. The only hope he had was to delay it for a while. Have you ever had the knowledge of something you dreaded but knew you had to do? When this happens to me, I try to think about anything else, no matter how odd, in order to distract myself from the inevitable. I get caught up in feelings or thoughts or ideas that I normally would avoid, all because of a vain hope that if I ignore something long enough it will go away. But Jacob was beginning to sense that he would never be rid of Destiny. He now felt this strange desire to have never left his home in the first place, for something inside of him knew that, whatever the reason, his destiny had been set.

Perhaps it was something he had done or something he had forgotten to do. But like some people, he was determined to avoid it for as long as possible. Then, fate dealt its hand. Or, should I say destiny?

Jacob felt as if his feet suddenly slipped beneath him, but he knew that it was not the case. The entire structure of the building began to shake. Hangings fell, tiles splintered, chairs toppled, and glass shattered. Then the floor of Mr. Brimmings' office split slowly in half. Jacob and Sylvia turned to see out the window an entire cityscape of structures collapsing. I will not describe it in vivid detail, or else I would have to use language and descriptive words that I often try to avoid. I will simply say that it was not a pretty sight. It was a sight that caused Jacob and Sylvia's hearts to sink into their stomachs.

Jacob had never been in an earthquake before, and he had imagined it to be rather different than it really was. He all at once decided that for his whole life he had taken the idea behind having one's feet on solid ground for granted. It was like an eerie vibration that sent itself up one side of the body and came back down through the other. Never in his life had he felt so disconnected from the horizon line and yet so connected to the planet earth. He suddenly felt as if he could feel the world as nothing more than a big round globe floating through space, doomed to crash into a larger object at any moment.

All of this occurred to him within seconds of realizing what was actually happening, and he quickly regained his reasoning. It was a second too late however, for as soon as he began to tighten his grip on Mr. Leach's invention, the half of the floor on which Sylvia stood ripped itself apart from the rest of the room and fell out of the side of the building so that the exterior wall was no more. The rupture jerked the invention from Jacob's hands and it went tumbling down the one-hundred and seventy-three stories along with Mr. Brimmings' big desk, two shelves worth of his expensive liquor, and a lot of his other really cool stuff.

It was solid luck that Sylvia was able to leap from the falling platform to the stable floor just in the nick of time. Jacob had been knocked flat on his back by the violent shaking, but he was soon up on his feet.

"You see," said the voice now entering the room once more, "It's only a matter of time." The children fought a frightening feeling, for the voice echoed to a dreadfully soothing rhythm in their minds, as if it were beginning to lull them asleep.

Jacob and Sylvia stepped back until there was no firm ground left on which to stand. Several hundred feet of falling debris and collapsing structures bustled beneath them. The darkness filled the hollow room. To the children, it seemed as if tentacles of smoke came hurling toward them, attempting to force them over the edge.

"Thank you," said Sylvia, looking up at Jacob. She had to look up into his eyes because he did happen to be slightly taller than she.

"For what?" Jacob asked, now more curious than frightened.

"For being such a friend," said Sylvia.

Sylvia knew that other than out of a sturdy moral obligation, Jacob really didn't have to treat her the way he did. She knew that most boys his age would have given into the more voracious draws of youth and adventure, such as running through fields and throwing sticks at birds, squashing bugs, or simply playing childish games. Jacob was different though. To Sylvia, it was almost as if she had grown into friendship with someone twice her age. She didn't know why exactly he still displayed such a strong willingness to care for her even through everything that had happened. She only wished she could see her father again and tell him how Jacob had lived up to the task he had been entrusted with.

Then, Jacob had an idea. He stepped in front of Sylvia and began to shout.

"You came for *me*, didn't you? Just leave her alone! I will go with you, but just leave her alone!"

Sylvia's thoughts were scattered as she tried to understand what Jacob was doing. Destiny changed its course as it lifted its icy hands toward Jacob. Just as he began to feel the chilling grip surge around his waist, Jacob heard a familiar voice.

"I found a balloon!" was the yell from out of the opening in the side of the building. "A balloon! It's brilliant!" shouted the voice once more.

"It's Mr. Brimmings!" shouted Sylvia, pointing out to Mr. Leach's balloon hovering next to where the big window had once been. "And it's Mary too!"

Mr. Brimmings brought the balloon to a halt as Mary tossed a rope to Sylvia, who quickly tied it around herself. She took the end and placed it in Jacob's hand.

Jacob had been dumbfounded at the sudden sight of Mr. Brimmings. Turning back toward Destiny, he gave a peculiar smirk that inspired an enraged jolt in the creature's disposition. The angel of darkness threw itself at Jacob as he and Sylvia fell slowly over the edge of the now crumbling tower. Hanging on as tight as one might in such a situation, they watched the remaining pieces of the tallest tower in the largest city dispel under the effects of apocalyptic distress.

"The city is gone," said Jacob, after He and Sylvia had joined Mr. Brimmings and Mary in the balloon. "It's just gone."

"At least we're free of that horrid creature," Sylvia replied, looking at Jacob and trying to guess his thoughts.

"No we aren't," he said, dismayed. "And we won't ever be. That thing isn't going to stop hunting me. It just isn't going to stop."

Sylvia looked out over the city and sighed. She wished she really were *as smart as all that*. Then perhaps she could think of something to say that would cheer them up.

Just then a horrible wind took hold of the balloon and cast it out to sea. Mr. Brimmings' attempts to fight the torrent were useless, for it raged on and on until there was no land left in sight. The night came in and Mr. Brimmings began to worry that the balloon was about out of fuel.

"Listen," he said, breaking the engaging conversation between Sylvia and Miss Mary Strubert. The pair had been chatting for who knows how long about who knows what, and Jacob had long since decided that he was asleep, even though he really wasn't.

"Listen! Do you hear that sound?" Mr. Brimmings spoke up once more. "I really think the fuel tank is just about empty."

"Do you suppose we could burn something else?" Mary asked.

"I doubt it," said Mr. Brimmings. "This tank is for propane only."

"Well, we can't land in the sea," remarked Sylvia. "That wouldn't do."

"No, that wouldn't do at all," agreed Miss Strubert, thoughtfully twirling her straw blonde hair with her dainty fingers. Then they broke off into another stint of dialogue entirely.

Mr. Brimmings and the now conscious Jacob looked at one another.

"Have you seen any land at all?" Jacob asked, standing up and surveying the protruding seascape.

"None," Mr. Brimmings replied, sighing and running his finger beneath his nose as to catch a sniffle.

"We could land on that cruise ship," said Jacob.

And that's exactly what they did. The last drop of fuel burned away just as the basket came to rest on the deck of the colossal cruise liner. To the passengers of the dwindling balloon, it seemed almost as if it were meant to happen.

Unbeknownst to Jacob, Sylvia, Mary, and Henry Brimmings, a crowd of onlookers gathered curiously along the deck, keeping their distance from the descending globular aircraft. The four friends exited the balloon to a surprisingly jovial greeting.

"Heroic Captain Rescues Struggling Balloon Enthusiasts!" shouted a rather cheery-mannered, overweight gentleman dressed unmistakably as, well, a sea captain. He had dark, thick curly hair that mingled almost indistinguishably with his unkempt eyebrows. His cheeks were red as cherries. Gold trimmings lined his white suit, and a small gold pin in the shape of a submarine stuck proudly from his lapel. He tipped his skippers cap and introduced himself.

"I'm Reginald Bing Bostwick!" he exclaimed, "And I just saved your lives. I'm the captain, by the way."

"You're the captain?" Sylvia asked amidst the rustle of people crowding about.

It seemed to Sylvia as if everyone was in dinner dress, gowned up properly for an evening meal. Jacob simply listed the crowd's strange attire into his mental directory of weird things adults sometimes do.

"Yes, my dear little lady. I captain this very vessel," Reginald Bostwick said, motioning to his first mate to hurry on over. "Come on! Come on! Grab a photo! Make sure you get my good side, and don't use the harsh flash."

Another gentleman slipped out of the crowd. "Captain, you just saved these poor helpless wanderers," he remarked, jotting something down in a small notebook. The man wore a plaid shirt, a pair of hiked-up suspenders, a felt coat, and a fedora that housed a white tag on which a word had been hastily scribbled. He scratched his small brunette mustache only once and then waited with pen in hand for the expectant reply.

"Why, yes, I certainly did," said the captain.

"I'm a reporter," said the man. "Let's hear the whole story."

"Well, I'm the captain," said the captain. "I spotted these young fellows struggling for life up in that blustery night air and I said, 'I ought to save those poor fellows.' Did I not say that, Julian?"

First Mate Julian gave a quick nod of the head. "Indeed. You said, 'I ought to save those poor fellows.' He certainly did."

"What else can you tell us?" asked the reporter, quickly scribbling a description of the four rescued passengers. The description of Jacob and Sylvia simply read, *two children, short.*

"Well, I'm the captain," said Captain Reginald Bostwick. "My full name is Captain Reginald Bing Bostwick. "I've been the captain for fifteen good years, I've got four captain's outfits, I have a grand collection of Irish battling tops, I own my very own submarine, and I'm not too bad at croquet."

"He does play a mean game of croquet," included Julian.

"So you steered the ship to catch us?" Sylvia piped up. "How thoughtful."

"Steered the ship?" asked Captain Bostwick. "No, I don't think I did that." He turned to Julian with a quirky drift between his eyebrows. "Julian, who steers the ship?"

"I'm not really sure," said Julian. "Should I take a note of it and find out at a later date?"

"Yes, please do. Take a note and find that out. It seems like it could turn out to be a valuable piece of information. For now, however, let us join our guests in the ship's fabulous dining hall for a feast. We must toast to their health and my bravery and a lot of other things I'll think up along the way." Captain Bostwick's tone lifted to an even higher level of elation and there began a sort of skip in his step as he thought about food.

Jacob and Sylvia held onto each other as they were escorted along the deck and into the dining hall. It was a superb facility, with round glass tables, elegant décor, a posh chandelier, four master staircases, and terraces surrounding the upper level.

Now, at this point, Jacob began to notice something very peculiar about the way the ship rocked back and forth. At first, due to the commotion about the deck, he had failed to realize the strange behavior of the boat, but as they made their way into the dining hall, it really became too obvious to ignore.

"Whoever is driving this boat is nuts," Jacob whispered into Sylvia's ear. "It keeps rocking one way, and as soon as I find my feet it rocks back the other."

"You're right," Sylvia agreed. "I bumped into one of those pillars on the way in and it hurt very badly."

"It will probably get better when we sit down to eat," Jacob remarked.

Despite Jacob's optimism, he was wrong. For as the captain cupped his hands together, initiating the round of appetizers, Jacob and Sylvia knew that they were in for a rough course. They felt their stomachs roll up and down in every which direction. As the table tilted back and forth, it was evident that the shrimp had no intention of staying on one's plate, and the scallops were even less likely to contain themselves. The electric eel also seemed to migrate back and forth throughout the entire meal. As he caught his own from enduring a nasty spill, Jacob motioned for the fifth time for Sylvia's glass to be refilled.

"Another glass for the young lady," the waiter announced. "You sure do know your wine."

"She isn't drinking it," Jacob complained. "It keeps spilling over with the rock of the boat."

"We're drinking wine?" Sylvia smirked, her eyes growing big and round and sparkling at the sight of another glass.

The waiter laughed. "No, madam. My apologies. I fear it is simply an expression."

Sylvia was too busy tasting the next glass to hear him. "Jacob, have you tried this stuff?" she asked. "My father never let me have it."

Jacob smiled. He laughed inside. Then he surveyed the tables of dining cruise-goers, wondering how anyone else managed to even get a bite to eat while enduring such an inconvenient sway.

"My crab is doing somersaults," he said to Sylvia, placing his head down on the table and letting out a sigh.

"Young man!" came a voice from across the table. "Who taught you table manners?"

Jacob looked up to see an elderly lady studying him through a pair of golden bifocals. Though she sported several layers of finery, her most interesting adornment to Jacob was most undoubtedly a single peacock feather, which sprung from her blue felt hat.

"My mother," Jacob replied.

"My mother, *madam*," the lady corrected, placing one finger up and shaking it side to side.

"Oh. Yes, madam," Jacob said with a blush of embarrassment at the fact that all the other persons at the table were now intently interested in their conversation.

Fortunately for Jacob, the woman changed the subject as quickly as she had introduced it. Turning her attentions to a solemn, darkly dressed individual who had said next to nothing since the beginning of the meal, she blabbered.

"Kelly, tell us what you were telling me earlier. You know, that bit about the illusiveness of proper arguments and such."

Kelly stroked his black mustache and slicked back his black hair. He placed one hand on the table and one on his hip. Taking the cigar from his lips, the man drew in a heavy breath. Anyone would have guessed him to be a silent type, of course they would have been wrong.

"Well," Kelly began. "Argumentation is an art, and art is by nature illusive. A proper argument, cleverly constructed, has little to do with being right. It has everything to do with brilliance of speech, deceptive strategy, and cheating. Let me show you what I mean."

As he spoke, his eyes brightened, and he made a flicking motion with his right index and middle fingers at the end of every point.

"If I decided to begin an argument with an undisclosed individual I shall simply refer to as Burks, then it would probably go something like so:

'I very much dislike you,' I would say.

'I beg your pardon,' Burks would reply.

You see, I am already fated to win the argument, for Burks already has no clue as to the fact that we are arguing.

Then, I would say, 'I very much dislike you, and for that reason I am going to continue this argument with you.'

'We were not arguing,' Burks would say, and of course he would be right, but I would never admit to it.'"

Kelly looked around at the guests. They pretended to be interested, but their confused stares revealed their aggravated state. Kelly quickly reasoned that his audience was not one for philosophical wanderings but rather more a lighthearted group, merry with the expectation of pleasant riddles and clever sentiments.

"Perhaps a line of verse instead," he proposed, lifting his chin up in the air and taking in another breath of introduction. "This is from one of my favorites," he spouted, reinvigorating his audience's appetite for his genial conversation. The single piece he quoted went like this:

Distance is a wonderful thing
It starves arguments and refreshes memories
It makes a heart sing in the middle of the night,
Teaching the world what it means to truly desire

Distance renews old partnerships
It folds the hands of competitors in friendship
Distance makes the heart yearn
For past times and better acquaintances

It fills one's mind with thoughts of wonder,
And makes you miss, really miss the one's you love
Distance is overpowering, really

"Brilliant!" the old lady with the single peacock feather spouted, joining the applause that encircled the table.

"Tell us the one about the sea vermin," came a voice from across the table.

Kelly, keen to keep the attention upon himself, complied without hesitation; he was altogether unaware of the mixed feelings that weighed upon the guests. Uneasiness blanketed the party, discounting two eager children and consequently one other – I specifically refer to the masked gentleman who had suggested the tale. Jacob and Sylvia were all ears. It's funny how a single piece of information, no matter how true, can change one's whole perception on life, truth, contentment, and unanticipated cruise-liner-hopping. It's also funny what happens when you drop a basket of eggs from an elevated point directly into some poor fellow's lap. Neither Jacob nor Sylvia would agree with the second point, but they were bound to witness the act eventually, I'm sure.

Actually, assuming you care, I will tell you a bit about the gentleman who sat at the end of the table. I'm talking about the one who suggested changing the topic to sea vermin. He wore a mask, and that's all you need to know. Everyone at the table had simply assumed he had mistaken the present evening for the evening prior, which had happened to be a masquerade party, one that Sylvia would have thoroughly enjoyed. And since he had (up to the point of mentioning sea vermin) failed to add any remark to the conversation, they had simply ignored him and gone about their dinners.

Kelly stood up, fashioning himself on one leg and resting the other on the seat of his chair. He began to tell the story.

"Seven weeks ago, in these very waters, a cruise vessel,

not too much different than this one, met with a terrible fate. Three vacationers escaped to tell the tale, and they each claimed that it happened late at night while they were preparing for bed. The trip had raised no problems up to that point, but that was soon to change. For as the evening settled down, they each began to feel a strong turbulence, almost as if something in the water circled the boat, brushing it's monstrous tentacles along the metal surface. Then, with a tremble that shook them each from their beds, the ship began to slow to a halt. Something was pulling it in the other direction. The passengers ran out on deck to catch sight of the monstrous beast, its limbs wrapped tightly around the back half of the boat and slipping along until the entire ship fell under the shadow of the infamous creature. The three that escaped just happened to survive the horrifying plunge as the monster yanked the ship down to the ocean floor. They were picked up days later, floating along a stretch of wood from the deck."

"What a horror!" exclaimed the lady with the peacock feather.

"What about the other ships?" the man with the mask inquired.

Almost everyone else at the table sneered unpleasantly in his direction. They each and every one of them knew all about the sea vermin and the lost ships, and they really did not desire to be reminded of such events. In their minds, it would be better if the subject simply evaded discussion altogether. However, no one commented on the matter for fear that they would inadvertently admit to their own lingering fears and imagined terror associated with such a fate.

"Every week since that first encounter seven weeks ago," Kelly began once more, "a similar occurrence has taken place. For seven weeks in a row, a single ship has disappeared into the depths of the sea, leaving behind no more than three survivors."

"You mean the sea vermin has swallowed seven

ships?" Jacob asked, beginning to get worked up over the story.

"Well, no," answered Kelly. "Technically, it has only eaten six ships. If it ate another this week, that would bring the count to seven."

Jacob looked around at the table full of passengers. Then he dropped any and all propriety and said something that he never would have normally let out of his mouth.

"What on earth drove you people to sign up for this cruise?" he asked, his voice almost squeaking from strain.

Kelly coughed, almost as if to muffle Jacob's brash comment. "Well, there is no proof that any such sea monster really does exist," he said. "Really, the chances are quite slim, considering no proper documentation has ever been recorded."

"What about the eye witnesses?" Jacob persisted.

"Mere fright and shock trauma," replied Kelly. "It really is nothing more than a story easily sold by newspapers – heightened rumors spread by harmless gossips."

"That's crazy," Jacob said, crossing his arms and readjusting his posture into a dull slump.

Those around the table piped in, agreeing wholeheartedly with Kelly. I suppose it can be dumb to admit to something potentially bad when you aren't forced to do so. At least, everyone at the table thought along such lines. Jacob and Sylvia looked down toward the man in the mask at the end of the table to see if he had something to say about the insolence they were presently witnessing. His seat was left empty, and the other guests were beginning to disperse as well.

As they were shown to their cabin, Jacob and Sylvia thought about Mr. Brimmings and Mary. Neither of the children had seen either of the couple in the dining hall, and to them it seemed odd. It should not have seemed too odd however, if they understood what it was like to be in love. Mr. Brimmings and Mary, helplessly attracted to one another, had spent the entire evening wandering around on deck, speaking passionately about all the things ordinary people who are in love speak about. I couldn't tell you what these things are, not because I have never been in love, but rather because I do not wish to spoil anything for you in case you have never walked in either Mr. Brimmings' or Mary's shoes.

Though you may think that a single day's time spent with a young lady is not near long enough for a gentleman to procure an engagement, I would disagree. And so would Mary, for at the same moment that Jacob and Sylvia began to discuss the absence of their two kind friends, Mary replied to the fateful question with a definite yes. Her positive response had something to do with Mr. Brimmings asking on such a magically bright evening. You see, the moon glowed almost supernaturally. It also had to do with the fact that she knew deep down that he was the only man for her.

Now I know that you may have a guess as to what was about to happen to Mr. Brimmings and Mary in only a short amount of time, but I need to let you know that you may be wrong. You see, everyone gets to that point where they can handle only so much of something. Even fortune seems to understand what it is like to face such a moment. With this in mind, I will tell you about the fate of the joyous couple.

Mr. Brimmings and Mary were so elated at the idea of getting married, that they first thought about asking the captain to marry them the next day. But there was just something about having Reginald Bing Bostwick expositing the words *I now pronounce you husband and wife* that did not sit well with the couple. Instead, Mary said that she had always dreamed of marrying in an old cathedral in Spain. Borrowing some fuel from the captain, they fired up the balloon and set sail through the night air. They had at first searched for Jacob and Sylvia in order to say goodbye, but being so deeply in love, they soon forgot what they were doing and made their way off into the evening sky. Unbeknownst to the sea vermin, an uncommon count of five passengers would survive that particular voyage. Three would be let live to tell the tale, and two would have left before the tale ever had time to be told.

"We'll see them tomorrow," Sylvia told Jacob, brushing and pinning her hair at the long sink in the stately bathroom. A true princess is never short of bobby pins.

The captain had seen to it that the children each received a grand quarters as accommodation for the remainder of the trip.

"I suppose," Jacob said, whiffing in a taste of night air at the circular cabin window. Though it seemed to him that Sylvia was probably right, Jacob couldn't help feeling that he was never going to see the two smitten friends again. "How much longer do you suppose this trip is going to last?" he asked, trying to find something else to talk about.

"I don't know," said Sylvia. "Of course, I've never been on a real boat before. Father used to always tell of his grand adventures out at sea as a young prince. One time he said that the best journey one could ever take is the journey home. I've never really known what he was talking about, though I think I'm beginning to understand. I would really like to go home again."

"I know you miss him," Jacob said, looking over at the hanging clock along the cabin wall. "It's late," he added.

"Where is your cabin?" Sylvia asked. "In case I need to wake you up for some reason."

"It's right next door," said Jacob, pointing to the wall behind Sylvia. "I will come over to check on you as soon as I awake, so please don't go wandering around without me in the morning."

"I won't," she said. "This place would be boring without you around anyway."

Jacob had almost stepped through the door when Sylvia caught him off guard.

"Jacob," she said.

"Yes?" he asked.

"Did your father ever tell you about his grand adventures from when he was younger?"

Jacob looked at his friend. She seemed so young for some reason, as if she were not as old as she had once been.

Then he told her.

"I never knew my father," he said. "He died before I was born."

Sylvia watched as Jacob's stare turned out across the cabin, almost penetrating the wooden walls and reaching over the sea. To Jacob, being a kid was one of the greatest things in the world, yet he couldn't help but hope that with every day he grew older, he would become a little more like his dad.

"I'm sorry," she said, sighing as comfortingly as she could.

"It's okay," he insisted, looking at her once more. "My mother used to tell me stories about him. I know he would have been a really great dad."

Jacob lay down in his bed seven minutes later, ready for a good night's sleep. Not even the strange tossing of the boat would bother him. Unfortunately though, he would not find any rest that night, for only a few minutes of peace would go by before all of hell would seem to reach up and take hold of the sleeping ship.

Jacob fell fast asleep, during which he dreamed a dream of past adventures and unfulfilled hopes. Then, just before he awoke, he dreamed that he and Sylvia sat on a park bench in a small clearing just down the road from his house. It was autumn and the crimson maple leaves were covering the short sidewalk to the bench. He felt the breeze of winter's eagerness across his freckled face. Then he looked over at her.

"I feel like someone is watching us," said Sylvia.

"I wouldn't know about that," said Jacob. "How come you left your home to come here? Won't your father be missing you?"

"Oh, I suppose so," she said, bobbing her head and lifting her shoulders. "But I can't stay here forever you know."

"I know," said Jacob. "I just wish there was some way that we could be together. I wish there was some way that we didn't have to leave one another. Life isn't fair."

"Life was never meant to be fair," she said, poetically.

"Then why does everyone pretend that it is?" Jacob

asked. "Everyone is always talking about getting what they deserve, whether for good or not so good."

"I don't think we get what we deserve," said Sylvia. "At least, not all of us. But even more so, I don't think we would want what we deserved if we got it. I think that some people are fine with accepting how things are, and others are not. Some people want to know what is really going on, but the problem with that is that it takes effort."

"Why do you have to leave?" Jacob asked again.

"I don't have to leave," Sylvia replied, placing her hand on Jacob's shoulder, her eyes full of meaning, "You do."

She stood up and crunched some leaves under her small feet. Then she kicked them up into the air and watched as they were carried away.

"I feel like someone is watching us," she said again.

Chapter 15: The Tiny Island

Jacob awoke to the sound of laughter outside his cabin door. Then he heard Sylvia's voice. To his tired ears, she sounded as if she was in an argument, so he hurried out. As he opened the door, he noticed the moon still hovered in a calm transcendence, only having migrated a few degrees toward the horizon. He must have only been asleep for half an hour or so.

"How can you possibly think this is a good idea?" she complained.

"Keep your voice down! They'll hear you," the bellhop shushed her.

"They ought to," said Sylvia in defiance.

Jacob and Sylvia's rooms were along a wooden walkway a few stories up from the deck. An awning hung out over part of the walkway, and it opened directly to the outside, revealing the sea and night sky. The bellhop, who stood a little taller and appeared to be several years older than both Sylvia and Jacob, leaned over the railing, holding something in his hand. Sylvia tugged on his shirt from behind.

"Sylvia, what are you doing?" Jacob asked, trying to see what it was the bellhop held over the edge.

"He's going to drop them!" Sylvia cried.

"What is it?" Jacob asked. "Who are you?"

"He's a terrible boy!" Sylvia hissed.

The bellhop turned around and opened the basket to where Jacob could see.

"It's just a practical joke," he said. "They won't do any harm."

Jacob peered into the basket where a dozen eggs nestled together neatly, and then he leaned over the railing and looked down. Asleep in a reclining chair along the deck below was a quirky gentleman with a newspaper draped across his chest and a bottle of something strong spilt on the bench next to him. Jacob recognized him as the reporter from earlier that evening.

"What a horrible joke," Jacob said, looking back at the boy and realizing his presumably cruel intentions.

"Look, the other lads have done this so many times, and it really isn't such a big deal. He'll just be in for a wicked surprise, that's all. I can't believe you two don't know a good trick when you see it."

"You aren't nice at all," Sylvia suggested, refusing to quell her protesting.

"We have to do something to keep ourselves entertained around here," the boy argued. "This place gets so dumb and boring after a while. You fellas are just a pair of lame toots. You're gonna get me caught anyhow."

The bellhop strolled quickly away, carrying the basket as if he had someone in particular to whom he needed to deliver it. Jacob was glad to see him go.

"I heard him out here laughing, so I thought I would come see what was going on," Sylvia explained.

"Well, I'm glad we stopped him before he splattered that poor man," Jacob replied. "Some people are so thoughtless. I know my mother would never allow it."

Some would hand it to fate that the two children

happened to be out and about at the particular moment in which they were, and others might call it a whim of chance. It may be wiser, however, to consider the pathways of providence, for so many others would not find similar good fortune while they slumbered away in their small cabin beds. It may not astonish you to learn that Jacob and Sylvia were suddenly cast against the railing by a jolt that seemed to ripple across the entire ship.

"Jacob, what was that?" Sylvia asked as she grabbed his shoulder for stability.

"I don't know," he said, even though in his mind he had a fairly good idea as to what had caused the shake. And unfortunately, if he had had taken the time to voice his guess, he would have been correct.

Then, it happened again, this time throwing the two children to the floor. Cabin doors along the walk began to open and some of the passengers began to step out and peer over the railing, mumbling to one another. The bellhop suddenly ran by, covered in egg drippings and crying heartily about being fraught with such a goopy happenstance.

"Let's go ask the captain!" Sylvia shouted, louder than she had expected to shout.

As Jacob stood back up, he looked at the troubled passengers, and then he looked out across the dark waters. He didn't really think talking to the captain would help anything. Instead he entertained the inclination that they just needed to leave. They needed to get off the ship, but he wasn't sure how.

"Okay, let's go," he said, shaking his head.

Jacob and Sylvia were soon lost in the tunnels below deck. They turned this way and then that, hoping to see someone they recognized. They were really hoping to randomly scuttle past a door labeled *Captain's Cabin*, but they found no such luck. Then the terrible shaking of the ship happened again. Then it happened again and again. Jacob felt as if his arms would unexpectedly fall out of their sockets, for each time the ship rumbled, he threw himself around Sylvia, keeping her from banging into the iron walls along the way.

Then a handful of sailors hurried past the two children, failing to notice their presence due to the urgency of their tasks, which I am sorry to say were soon to become completely meaningless. As they shuffled past, Jacob and Sylvia were forced into an open hatch in the wall of the minute hall. Before they could leave, a round iron door sealed shut before them.

Have you ever felt as if your circumstances decided themselves, almost as if they were meant to happen? Jacob and Sylvia held no present inclination as to this being the case, but they should have – considering what had happened to them so far. Little did they know that they had just entered the only part of the ship bound to survive the fateful attack.

"What in blazes!" hollered a thundering voice from behind them. "What are you doing in here?"

Jacob and Sylvia turned around to find Kelly standing over them in the small compartment with a large wrench in his hand.

"We're sorry," said Jacob. "We were looking for the captain's cabin and we got lost."

"No matter," Kelly replied, settling into what looked to be a cramped little driver's seat.

"What is this place?" Jacob asked. "There's not even enough room to stand up in here."

Just then, a loud banging rattled the round door that had slammed behind them. Soon the children could hear the frigid voice of the captain on the other side.

"You're in my submarine! That's my submarine and I order you to vacate! Open this door at once!" he yelled, his fury engulfing the brink of courtesy.

Just then, the cranking and rumbling of an engine surged around the compartment. The submarine lit up in various places, the glass windows near the front of the vessel slid open, and what seemed to be a broken voice began to say something indistinguishable.

"Sorry, mate," Kelly shrugged, refusing to look his accuser in the eye. "She's on autopilot. I've no idea how to stop her."

"You can't take my submarine!" the captain squawked again. "I'm Captain Reginald Bing Bostwick and that's my submarine!"

"You've got to let him have his submarine back," Sylvia begged, tugging on the sleeve of Kelly's jacket. "It isn't right to take things that don't belong to you."

"It isn't right to drown with the sinking ship either," said Kelly. "If he had been a better captain, perhaps we wouldn't be in this mess!"

"What mess?" Jacob asked, having a fairly good idea as to what Kelly referred.

"The sea vermin is about to swallow this ship," Kelly related, pausing to catch the looks on the children's faces.

"What?" Sylvia gasped. "We've got to do something."

"I *am* doing something," Kelly replied. "I'm getting out of here."

"You're taking my submarine!" the captain shouted from behind the locked door.

"You could at least let him in," Jacob cried, attempting to reason with Kelly.

Then, Jacob remembered Mr. Brimmings and Mary.

"Wait, we can't leave!" he shouted, pulling on Kelly's other sleeve. "Our friends are still on the ship. You have to let me find them!"

"It's too late," Kelly remarked, letting out a sigh of what could possibly have been apologetic remorse. "We're away."

He was right. A hatch opened before them and the little submarine propelled quickly through and out into the black waters. The light cast only a steady beam onto the darkness, revealing a wave of thick nothingness. Then, they saw it. A giant purple tentacle at least twice the width of the submarine slithered out of the darkness and right in front of their path.

"Good grief!" Kelly shouted.

Sylvia screamed and slid behind Jacob. Then the submarine began to surface. As they came to water level, the two disheartened children placed their faces up against the concave glass, each breath fogging their line of sight. The sub tossed gently in the night waves, silent with a small motor and three motionless passengers. Then, the cruise liner began to suddenly alter its course. As it decreased speed, it seemed to the children as if the boat were lifting up on its back end. The entire ship moved as a monster on its own, breaking the water in bursts of impressive power. The metal linings shuttered, and a piece of engineering ripped through the deck. Something was crushing the ship from beneath the surface. Then ten tentacles, each the size of an ordinary neighborhood lane, slithered out of the water, ran up all sides, and entangled themselves around the superstructure. It was certainly a sight.

The two children could but stand and observe as the hands of death crunched the boat straight down the middle. The bridge, the hull, the control room, the cabins, the shops, the pools, the spas, the libraries, the cinemas, the lounges, the dining halls, the gyms, the skating rinks, the jogging tracks, and even the golf courses were all drawn into the sea. Waves crashed and a whirlpool formed, and where the ship once had sat, there was only emptied ocean.

Jacob thought about the mammoth vessel sitting on the bottom of the ocean, wasting away year after year in a watery grave. Then, as if something sharp seemed to prick him from the inside, he remembered Mary and Mr. Brimmings.

"We have to do something!" he shouted, banging on the glass as hard as he could with both fists. "Our friends are still on the boat!"

"Oh my goodness," Sylvia gasped, losing her breath as she spoke.

"I'm afraid there isn't anything we can do," Kelly attempted to console the children. "That wave certainly won't let us get near the wreckage."

And he was right. The strange effect of the sudden immersion was a rising wall of water, which suddenly hauled them out across the sea, taking Kelly, Jacob, and Sylvia far away from where the boat had sunk. Then, when they thought that they could go no further, the submarine ran aground.

They crash-landed on a tiny island that seemed to be alone in the great sea. They each climbed out onto the shore and stood staring out at the endless expanse of water. There was nowhere for them to go, for the island was only about the size of an ordinary country cottage, and nothing rested on its surface but layers of sand.

Then, they all fell asleep. Do you ever feel like crying yourself to sleep? Well, Jacob had felt like doing so, but he found himself falling far too quickly. Sylvia as well had felt the urge to let out a good cry, but she too could not keep her eyes open long enough. They each slept, feeling as if nothing bad had ever happened, and then, right before they opened their eyes, sorrow began to inundate their subconscious minds.

Jacob awoke first, and then Sylvia. Kelly had long since been awake, and he had spent a good deal of the day attempting to launch the submarine back into the water. The two children looked at the sky. It was already evening again.

"Why is it so late? Jacob asked, wondering how it was that he managed to sleep through the entire day.

"I have no idea," Kelly replied. "It has been like this all day. The light has not changed since I awoke."

Sylvia stared off into the sunset, wondering if the celestial being were really moving or if her imagination simply tricked her into thinking so. Then, she began to cry. Jacob put his arms around her and squeezed her tight, hoping that she would not notice that he also cried with her. Then, the two children sat down in the sand and watched as the waves toppled on the shore.

"Why is life so terrible?" Sylvia asked, hoping that Jacob would somehow have the answer to a question she had asked herself so many times before.

"I don't know for sure," said Jacob. "I used to think I knew everything but now I'm sure I don't. There are so many things I don't know."

He brushed his cheek, thinking as hard as he could for an answer.

"Perhaps," he began, "life is so hard because we make it that way. We always blame other people for what they have done to us, but then we turn around and do the same thing to someone else. I guess we've missed the point. I feel like love may have something to do with what life was originally intended for, but I think love is most of the time misunderstood. Maybe if we listened to what love is trying to tell us, then we wouldn't have to make the same mistakes over and over and over."

"But everyone falls in love and it never helps anyone," said Sylvia.

"I'm not talking about falling in love," said Jacob, trying to explain a feeling he believed to be above him. "I'm talking about real love. Haven't you ever had someone in your life who was willing to give up everything simply because they loved you?"

Sylvia immediately thought about her father. Then she thought about someone else.

"What if we were able to love everyone like that?" Jacob asked, quickly letting his mind wander across the horizon, wishing he would catch site of his mother on her way to save him.

"But we can't," said Sylvia. "No one can do that."

"I know," he replied, almost laughing out a smile as he looked Sylvia in the eyes. "But I have a feeling that is what we were intended to do."

Just then, Kelly called Jacob's name, asking him for a hand with the submarine. Jacob got up and went over to help. Sylvia simply sat in the sand, thinking about what Jacob had said.

"I wish most things had never happened," she thought. Then, she looked up at what had appeared to be a figure walking across the water. He had only been in focus for a second, and then he seemed to disappear. She squinted and thought that perhaps it was… But then she reasoned that it couldn't be.

Jacob and Kelly pushed and shoved, moving the submarine the last few inches into the water until it sank down into place. Kelly climbed up into the hatch and checked to make sure the machine would still run. Then he let out a frightened cry.

"What is that?" he gasped, looking over to where Sylvia had sat.

Jacob turned around, not knowing what Kelly could have been making such a fuss about. Then, he saw it as well.

Have you ever wished to never see someone again, thinking that by you not seeing them they would cease to exist and therefore cease to have any effect on you? Well, Jacob, subconsciously at best, had hoped for such a miracle. But sadly, Destiny lingers on.

The cold creature stood directly behind Sylvia, who stood at the far end of the tiny island, frozen. She was looking at Jacob, but she knew exactly whom it was that stood over her. She suffered the cut of his icy breath. The sand around her had also turned black, and the darkness grew out toward Jacob.

Kelly started the engine and began backing up into deeper water. Jacob looked over at him and then to Sylvia. The creature Destiny clasped his arms around the child and began to pull her into himself.

"Come on!" Kelly shouted. "We have to get out of here! She is lost to us!"

Jacob sneered at Kelly, and then he realized how his arms shook. He was about to have to make a choice. He would either leave Sylvia and save himself, or he would stay on the island and attempt to rescue her from Death's hand. Though, it would be a rescue unlike any other, for Jacob knew that even if he could get her free, he would himself never be free from the creature. In the end, it was an easy choice to make, because some choices are not made right away, but rather through the slow sifting of time day after day.

Jacob tossed sand up behind him as he ran. As soon as Kelly realized what Jacob was doing, he closed the hatch and departed into the sea. It only took a few good strides before Jacob found himself face to face with the deadly angel. Without losing speed, he leapt up into the air and stretched himself out, flying madly into the creature Destiny.

"Let her go!" he screamed, fighting through the misty darkness with all his heart.

Taking a step back, the creature gathered its fierceness for a counter attack that cast Jacob down into the sand. Jumping up, he propelled himself into the darkness once more. He grasped Sylvia's hand and pulled as hard as his small body would let him pull.

"Give her back!" he screamed, setting his foot firmly in the sand and leaning all his weight away from the deadly being. He gritted his teeth and pulled. Then, with one final yank, Sylvia was loosed from the creature's grasp. Both children landed in the sand, their backs soaked and covered with the foaming of the waters. Jacob stood up and made a fist at his side.

"You can take me with you, but just let her go," he said. "I'll go with you if you just stay away from her."

"I cannot stay away forever," Destiny replied. "Some things are just meant to be. Death is something that no man or woman can evade. One day everyone must die."

"Why does it have to be today?" Sylvia asked, standing to her feet and swallowing a frightening thought.

"Today is what was written," Destiny said, still fixing his gaze on Jacob. "It's time to go," he said, holding out his hand to the young boy.

Jacob looked over at Sylvia. He thought about her father and how he had failed to bring her back to him. He thought about his life up to that point. Then, he thought about leaving.

"Sylvia," he said. "I can't stay with you forever. I want

to, but I just can't."

"But where are you going?" she asked. "Where is he taking you?"

"He's taking me home," said Jacob, glancing over at his patient pursuer.

"Home to your house?" Sylvia asked.

"No," Jacob replied. "He's taking me to a different home – a new home." He voice was calm now, and it had lost its touch of sadness.

"But I want you to stay," Sylvia began to pout. "I don't care where he wants to take you. He can't have you."

"I must," Destiny whispered. "It is for each man to die at his appointed time." Staring deeply into Jacob's soul, he said, "Jacob, it is time."

Then, Jacob forgot about Sylvia. He forgot about life and love and happiness. He forgot about the future. Things like kindness, hope, beauty, and friendship pervaded his stream of consciousness and his way of being. All thoughts of peace dripped from his changing heart as he took his first step toward Destiny.

Sylvia watched as he seemed to walk out of existence and into another world. His body left itself at the curtain of time and he felt nothing any longer. Only a vast emptiness held onto his wandering soul.

Now, I know you may feel that Jacob did not deserve such an end. But I need to remind you of two things. First, I told you that Jacob would eventually be overcome by destiny. I let you know about his eventual demise, and so you have little (if any) right to be upset. Perhaps I should have said it a few more times so that you would have believed it, or perhaps a few times fewer. Either way, you knew what was going to happen from almost the beginning. Second, people don't deserve to live. No one deserves the life they have been given. Life is a gift. It is a gift that we often fail to be thankful for. We fail to be thankful for our own lives, and perhaps we often consequently undervalue the lives of others. A life ought to be the most valuable possession we can fathom, but so often we treat one another in such a way that the very opposite would seem true. When we undervalue life, we lose out on any of its real benefits. One thing I can tell you is this: Jacob understood what it meant to value someone. He did.

Chapter 16: Going Home

There are times when even the thing we love the most has to leave. There are times when no matter how badly we wish, we cannot stop someone we love from going away. Such is the case with Jacob finding his destiny. He lived and loved and now it was time for him to go. As I said before, there isn't anything that can stop destiny. There isn't anything that can prevent its destructive nature.

Jacob and Sylvia stayed exactly where they were for a little while as I thought about what I had just said. I thought and I thought. Then, I knew what had to happen.

Just then, Dawson Quinn appeared on the beach. His feet sunk down into the sand and he smiled when Sylvia saw him.

"Dawson!" she cried. "Thank goodness! Quickly, we need your help!"

"What is the matter, child," he asked, walking over to her and kneeling down. He placed his hand on her shoulder and gave her another smile. To Sylvia, he seemed taller and yet even gentler than before.

"Death is taking Jacob away!" she said, pointing to where Jacob was almost invisible – his life being drawn away in a mist of cloud.

"Destiny, is this true?" Dawson asked, standing boldly to his feet.

"It is," said Destiny.

"He's evil," said Sylvia. "He doesn't care about anything except death."

"He isn't evil, child," Dawson explained. "He simply is what he is. Everyone, in their current state, is meant for death one day. Destiny is simply doing what he was made to do."

"How can you say that?" Sylvia asked, folding her arms and looking angrily at Dawson. This was the first time she felt as if he spoke against her.

"I say it because it's true," said Dawson.

"But he's my friend, and I love him," said Sylvia, letting a tear run from her face and mix with the moist sand.

"Cheer up, child," said Dawson. "That is why I am here. I came to save him."

"Then do something," Sylvia pouted once more. "He's almost gone."

Dawson sighed a great sigh and began to speak with Destiny.

"What is the price for a such a child?" he asked.

"A soul is of great worth," replied Destiny. "A life for a life, my friend."

"What does that mean?" Sylvia asked, looking up at Dawson, who now proceeded to roll up his sleeves.

He clasped her hand for a moment. "Do you want to go home?" he asked.

"Yes, very much so," Sylvia replied.

"Then it shall be so," said Dawson. "But you must say goodbye to Jacob, for he must too go home for a while."

"Okay," said Sylvia, drying her tears and giving him as good of a smile as she could muster.

Then, Dawson stood up and faced Destiny with both

feet forward. He gently walked into the darkness, leaving his one existence behind. Though Sylvia looked for him, she could not see him. All she could see was black. Then, Jacob stepped out of the darkness and found his footing on the shore. Destiny wrapped his arms into himself and began to collapse into a fade of mist. The blackness subsided and death shrank back into the heart of the sea, leaving the two children on the tiny island.

A cloud, much like one they had seen before, developed out of thin air and picked them both up in a whirlwind. They spun through the shroud of rushing air until they came to rest on the balcony outside King Fredrick's room. As Jacob realized where they had come to be, he wondered why Sylvia cried so helplessly.

"What is it?" he asked.

"He's gone," she replied through her sobs.

"Who's gone?"

"Dawson. Dawson is gone."

"What do you mean he's gone?" Jacob asked, for he had no knowledge of Dawson Quinn ever being present on the island.

"He went with that horrible creature. He went with it, so that you wouldn't have to."

Jacob looked down at the marble tiling on the floor. He had seen a shadow of someone he once knew in passing through the mist, but he had no idea that it could have been Dawson Quinn.

"Jacob," began Sylvia. "He took your place."

Jacob looked away and stepped over to the edge of the balcony. Placing his elbows on the parapet, he sunk his chin into his hands and stared off into the forest. He thought about how he had not trusted Dawson when he met him. He thought about what he had said to him. Then he thought about the deep darkness from which he had been suddenly drawn up.

"It was so cold in there," said Jacob. "It was so cold," he said again, beginning to cry. He looked over at Sylvia.

"Oh, Jacob," she said, running over to give him a great big hug.

They shed a few tears together as if they had always known one another and nothing more needed to be said. Then it was time to say goodbye.

"You're going home now, aren't you?" Sylvia asked, wiping her eyes clean.

"Yes. I've got to return to my mother," Jacob replied, doing the same.

"Well, don't stay away too very long."

"I won't," he promised.

They hugged once more, and then Sylvia stepped through the curtain and into her father's room. Without hesitation, King Fredrick threw his arms around her, pulling her off her feet and giving her a joyous spin. She at once began to tell him stories from her ventures. They laughed and Jacob watched from the balcony. Then, just as the whiff of cloud reappeared to take him away, King Fredrick peered out at him. He gave Jacob a simple nod, as if to say, "Well done, son." And with that Jacob was swept away.

He had only traveled for a few seconds when all of a sudden he found himself standing in his own bedroom, with everything just the way it was before. The tree that had grown through his ceiling had vanished, the cracks in the floor and walls were all gone, and his fish was swimming about as if nothing had happened at all. The only thing out of place was that the fish bowl only seemed to be half way full.

"Well, you won't survive long in that," said Jacob, unwittingly speaking to his fish. "Let's find you some water."

Pushing open the window panel, Jacob held the bowl out in the steady pouring rain until it was full to the top. Then he set it down again on the shelf and looked down into the water.

"Do you suppose I shall ever see her again?" he asked.

The fish simply swam one way and then the other. Then, Jacob heard his mother entering by the kitchen door downstairs. She called to Jacob to help her unload the groceries in the rain.

"I've got to go," said Jacob. "I hope I see her again."

With that, he leapt up onto both feet and ran out of his room and downstairs. On his way, he gave the dog a good pat on the head.

"I hope *so*," said the fish.

THE END.

Look for these other titles from Inspire Christian Books

My Mess by Troy Black

Jacob & Sylvia II by Troy Black

Morning By Morning by Sister Clara Payne

ABOUT THE AUTHOR

Troy Black lives with his wife, Leslie, in south Texas. He likes board games, playing sports, fishing, and going for long walks. Troy and Leslie have a daughter named Mirabelle.

Troy and his wife started Inspire Christian Books out of a passion to spread the Gospel and the Truth of God's Word. It is their desire to see those who are lost come to salvation in Christ Jesus, and for the Christian church to experience an awakening through the work of the Holy Spirit.

If you are interested in having Troy speak at a Christian event or conference, or for other inquiries, you can contact him through InspireChristianBooks.com.

LOOKING TO PUBLISH YOUR BOOK?

Do you have a Christian fiction or non-fiction book that you would like to see published? Find our publishing information and guidelines on InspireChristianBooks.com. We can't wait to read your work.

Made in the USA
Lexington, KY
01 May 2017